## The crowd went wild, screaming "Go, go, go!" as if they were at a sporting event.

Only one person in the world could inspire that kind of crazed response.

I thought I knew her, but this time my cousin Courtney had gone to new heights. She was always springing new talents on me. Hidden accomplishments. This time she had sprinted up a tree faster than lightning.

Jolly's trainer was trying to pull Jolly away from Courtney, who was at the top of the tree hanging on and hugging him.

Courtney may love animals, but this was going too far. She was now feeding Jolly clumps of leaves. It was love at first sight.

I looked up and up and up at Courtney, who wasn't budging. Neither was Jolly. The fire department had been called and, after they arrived, they ran around trying to find the best spot for a net in case Courtney fell or decided to jump. But common sense should have told everyone that if Courtney got up, she could get down.

It was Jolly the giraffe they had to worry about.

His trainer couldn't pry him away from Courtney. They had fallen in love.

**Books by Judi Miller**

My Crazy Cousin Courtney
My Crazy Cousin Courtney Comes Back
My Crazy Cousin Courtney Returns Again
My Crazy Cousin Courtney Gets Crazier

Available from MINSTREL Books

# Judi Miller

MY CRAZY COUSIN COURTNEY

GETS CRAZIER

A MINSTREL® BOOK

Published by POCKET BOOKS
New York   London   Toronto   Sydney   Tokyo   Singapore

A MINSTREL PAPERBACK *Original*

 A Minstrel Book published by
POCKET BOOKS, a division of Simon & Schuster Inc.
1230 Avenue of the Americas, New York, NY 10020

ISBN: 0-671-00279-1

First Minstrel Books printing February 1997

10  9  8  7  6  5  4  3  2  1

A MINSTREL BOOK and colophon are registered trademarks of
Simon & Schuster Inc.

Cover art by Carla Daguanno

Printed in the U.S.A.

*For Renée Cho and J & A
(otherwise known as Jean and Alan)*

GETS CRAZIER

# CHAPTER ═══ ═══ ONE

The first few days of school were almost sacred to me. Getting my classroom assignment, twirling the combination on my brand-new lock, pasting posters on the inside of my locker, and feeling organized were traditions I loved.

It was hard to believe summer had flown by and my cousin Courtney (My Crazy Cousin Courtney) was on her way, in a jumbo jet, back to Beverly Hills, California, to attend what she referred to as "ugh school." I had been sorry to see her go two hours ago at JFK International airport. It was a tearful parting. In fact, I missed her already, but not more than I was looking forward to getting some boring normalcy back into my life. Courtney could be, well, unpredictable.

1

Looking down at my desk as I sat in its matching chair, I picked up my shiny new green ruler and fingered my blue binder with the multicolored dividers I had neatly lettered. One was for English, another for history, one for algebra, and the fourth was for French. I was also taking art and gym. My mom had embroidered my name, Cathy Bushwick, on my sweatshirt for gym. But most exciting of all was that I would be playing the cello in Mr. Korda's orchestra.

I opened the door to my closet, where I had neatly hung all the new school clothes my mom and I had bought. A blue- and green-plaid pleated skirt and a lilac angora sweater, a crisp white blouse (I loved white blouses), new designer jeans, a flannel shirt, new sweats, new sneaks, and a red silk dressy dress with a large sash. Suddenly I wished Courtney were here to reassure me I would wear it to a party soon.

I didn't know when I would hear her voice again, but I knew what she would say. "Cathy, relax. You're such a worrywart. You'll wear the dress. Trust me."

I heard the phone ringing, interrupting my daydreams, and heard my mom yelling, "Cathy, it's for you!"

I wondered who it could be. None of my friends were back from their summer vacations yet. Felicity was visiting her cousins in Ireland, and Dawn was in Cincinnati, Ohio.

"It's Courtney," my mom said, handing the phone to me.

I looked at my watch, screaming, holding the phone like a hot potato. What had happened this time? Had she been hijacked? Had she missed her plane? Anything was possible. Courtney would not easily relinquish her title of My Crazy Cousin Courtney.

"Don't worry, Courtney, you've been in worse jams, and besides, it will be good publicity for your movie," I said before saying "hi." My cousin Courtney was a real live movie star. She had recently appeared in *The Laundry Bag Murders* directed by Cliff Carothers, who had once been a famous soap star until Courtney suspected him of committing a murder, which of course he hadn't, and in turn making him a celebrity. Well, anyway, that's a little of what she's like.

"Cath," she said. "I'm calling from the plane." Then I heard her instructing the flight attendant. "I'll have both the chicken and the fish dinners." Good old Courtney. She could eat all day and never gain an ounce. Of course, she did burn up a lot of calories thinking up ways to get into trouble.

"Cathy, I'm coming back to New York!"

"What!" I said, jumping up and down, even though I felt a strange sensation in the pit of my stomach. Dread. Then an immediate feeling of guilt. She was my second cousin and my best friend, but she was also crazy.

"I got a job. Mrs. Phillips is the most awesome agent in the world. She's super!"

I imagined Courtney sitting on the plane, the cellular phone attached to her ear as if she were an alien. Well, some very beautiful alien. It would give all the other passengers a chance to stare at her, at her emerald green eyes, curly coppery hair, and peaches-and-cream complexion.

"I'll have more salad dressing," I heard her say.

"What job?" I demanded.

"Oh, chocolate ice cream," she said between bites.

"Courtney, finish your dinner before starting on your dessert." She ate too fast. She always ate too fast.

"No, that's the name of the movie. *Chocolate Ice Cream.* It's a feel-good romantic comedy to be shot in New York this fall. And I have a starring role. I play the daughter of a private eye. My mom, I mean Joan, just called and talked to your mom before I called you, and it's okay for me to stay with you. It will be the same as this summer."

I shut my eyes, trying to forget the summer. "But what about school?" I asked.

"More butter, please. Oh, yeah, " 'ugh school.' Well, I have to go, but my mom, I mean Joan, says not the whole day. Only in the afternoons."

Again that sinking feeling. "But, Courtney, what school? A private school?"

"Oh, no. I think they're making arrangements to send me to your school, Cath." I thought of my shiny ruler, my new blue binder with the dividers, my lilac angora sweater. School. And into school would come

4

the three-ring circus that was my crazy cousin Courtney's trademark. I wondered what Intermediate School 44 would think of her when she arrived with no less force than a tornado.

She would get us into trouble. She always did. She generated her own publicity tornado, but this time it would blow all over school. I was shy. How could I hold my head up if everyone knew my name?

"So I'll land in Beverly Hills, pick up some clothes while the script is FedExed to me. Then I'll hop back on a plane. Isn't that super? I hope Joan's right that I'll only have to go to school in the afternoons."

I.S. 44 would never be the same, I was sure of that. "Yeah, it's super," I said softly. "Courtney, you're going to be awfully busy," I said, hoping she might consider going to a private school. "It's a lot of responsibility. Working in the morning, 'ugh school,' I mean school, in the afternoon." Even with that much to do, Courtney would still find time to get us into trouble. Trouble followed Courtney as leaves were lifted in the wind.

I could see it all now. We would end up at a precinct house, and Mom and Howard, my stepfather, would have to come rescue us, my mom with only one earring on and frantic and Howard cracking up with laughter. Good old Courtney would pose and smile for the cameras as someone ordered out for pizza or doughnuts. All this during a school year? At least during the summer we could keep her outrages kind of semiprivate.

I couldn't see Courtney, but I knew what she looked like right then and how she was gesturing. She would be waving me away.

"I can tell you're worried about me, Cathy. You're always worrying. I'll be able to manage school and my movie. Don't worry."

Courtney was coming back.

Just then my mom took the phone away from me and said, "Congratulations, Courtney. Now, pack warm stuff and tell Joan to get you some vitamins. Oh, you're going to buy all new winter clothes? I hope you can find the time to shop. Your schedule will be backbreaking. Yes, Courtney, yes, Courtney, yes, Courtney."

I found my way into the room that was still "just my room" with its white twin beds and pink- and white-sprigged bedspreads. For a second I felt light-headed. As Courtney would say, maybe I had swallowed some gum and it was gumming up the works. Courtney was really coming back to do another movie. Of course I was thrilled for her. But then why did I feel so blue? Truthfully I felt like crying.

I noticed my mom in her pink pantsuit standing in the doorway watching me.

"So, Courtney's coming back."

"Yeah, isn't that terrific, Mom. We'll have a lot of fun. Just like this past summer."

"Don't worry, Cathy," Mom said, immediately understanding how I was feeling. Courtney won't have time to get into trouble. Look at her schedule." Of

6

course my mom thought she was right, but I knew in my heart that Courtney could always find time for trouble, school year or not. All I aspired to was to become an invisible student at I.S. 44, but I didn't have a chance with Courtney. She would make us stand out like neon signs.

On the other hand, with Courtney around, I always had more confidence and courage.

My mom, who was great, came over and gave me a big hug. "It'll be okay, Cathy. After all, we can't send her to a hotel."

I thought of the coming school year. Courtney would film in the mornings. What I never understood was how she memorized all her lines, how she cried on cue with people watching her, how she became another person. But it was the afternoons I was afraid of.

What would she do then? Blow up the school!

# CHAPTER ════ ════ TWO

I had a strange sense of déjà vu, the feeling that I had been there before. And actually I had. Three months ago Mrs. Phillips, Courtney's agent; Howard, my stepfather; and my mom had gone with me to pick Courtney up at the airport. Courtney had been missing then and was missing now. She hadn't gotten off the plane with the other passengers again.

None of the airline personnel knew what had happened. Neither did we. There we all were at JFK International, one of the largest airports in the world waiting for a no-show, five-foot, ninety-pound girl with coppery curls and flashing emerald eyes. The last time this had happened Howard suggested that Courtney wanted to make a dramatic entrance. She had.

She came gliding in on one of those mini-trucks surrounded by tons of luggage holding Wilheim Von Dog, who was wearing heart-shaped red-sequined sunglasses that matched Courtney's. Those glasses were her trademark. Her signature sunglasses. I often suspected she had at least twelve pair made up at a store in Hollywood or Beverly Hills. Once she lost a pair but produced another instantly.

As I looked around I decided I had never seen so many people in one place. Surely one of them had to be my cousin Courtney, or should I say, my crazy cousin Courtney.

"Maybe we should call her parents in California," Mrs. Phillips said, checking her watch nervously. "Her plane landed forty-five minutes ago."

"Courtney!" my mom screamed with relief, and we all turned to her. She was gazing at a girl who was looking up and trying to get her luggage off the baggage carousel. The girl was almost a double for Courtney, but only almost. No one could look like Courtney.

As it turned out, Courtney happened to be the girl's name. We all stared in amazement as she said, "Have we met?"

My mom slinked away just in time to hear Howard say, "Well, I for one think Courtney is somewhere in the airport but just wants to make an entrance, you know, something different."

How different could she get?

What had she planned this time?

I shut my eyes. The most dramatic and impulsive thing I had ever done was cut my hair. I used to wear it in one long braid hanging down my back, but Courtney inspired me to cut it off. It was a really big deal to me because I had had that braid for so long a time.

I was missing orchestra orientation to pick Courtney up, and she wasn't even here. At orientation we were supposed to get our instruments and even begin to play a little. I was eager to learn the cello. Orchestra would be my kind of activity, where no one had to be a leader.

As I searched for Courtney, swiveling my head from side to side like a windshield wiper, I marveled again at how the two concepts, school and my crazy cousin Courtney, just didn't mesh.

I almost forgot that the scene at the airport this time was a little different from last time. Felicity and Dawn had come with us this time. They were awe-struck at meeting a movie star. (They should try living with one, I thought.)

My mom liked to refer to Felicity and Dawn, my two closest friends (not counting Courtney, who was in a class by herself), as the Odd Couple. Felicity was very tall and skinny and I thought she looked like Olive Oyl from the Popeye cartoons. Dawn was short and chubs, but very cute.

"Wow, does your cousin Courtney always leave you waiting like this?" Felicity asked. "That's so Hollywood."

"Yes," Dawn agreed. "But it's bad for her image."

"Yes." Felicity nodded fiercely. "Now that she's about to become this really huge movie star, you have to help create an image for her."

I smiled and gritted my teeth, which was a bad habit of mine. I would have gladly traded in Courtney's present image for anything they could think up.

Mrs. Phillips returned from studying the TV that announced arrivals and departures for the fourth time. "Her plane definitely landed," she said. I could tell she was worried.

"Image is everything," Felicity said, continuing her own conversation.

"If you don't have image, you really don't have anything," Dawn said. Actually, they always agreed on everything. I thought of orchestra orientation, and I guessed it would have been over by then. It would have been so comforting to hold my bright, shiny cello, tune it, put resin on the bow, and make music. We just had to get over this latest Courtney hurdle— we had to find Ms. Courtney Green in mammoth JFK airport. All at once I got an inspiration.

"Let's page her! Maybe she's lost." Well, I doubted that, but at least we'd let her know that we knew she was there. Whatever she had planned for a spectacular entrance would have to be postponed. She couldn't pile all her luggage in one of those little trucks and ride through the airport waving like the First Lady or the President of the United States.

11

We all decided paging her was the best choice.

Felicity added, "And everyone in the airport will hear her name over the loudspeaker."

"Good for the image," Dawn said. Felicity nodded.

As we were trying to locate the lady who did the paging, we couldn't believe what we heard.

"Courtney Green, paging Courtney Green, please proceed to the information booth. Paging Courtney Green." Someone was paging Courtney. Mrs. Phillips was her only agent. Courtney was staying with us. Felicity and Dawn hadn't even met her yet. So it was none of us. But there was her name being blared all over JFK. "Paging Courtney Green. Will Ms. Courtney Green please proceed to the information desk." We all stood thunderstruck.

Were there two Courtney Greens? Someone wanted Courtney. What could she have done now? But I knew my cousin Courtney.

Wouldn't it be crazy . . . no, it was unthinkable, but funny. What if Courtney had paged herself?

"What if she's paging herself?" I blurted out. I could never keep my thoughts secret. I could never tell a lie, either.

"But that doesn't make any sense," Felicity said.

"None at all," Dawn agreed.

I nodded. Courtney never made any sense. This was how she planned to top herself. She couldn't just make an entrance.

We arrived like a six-person amoeba at the information desk.

"Someone paged Ms. Courtney Green?" Howard asked as if he were Courtney.

"We're looking for her. Someone paged her," Mrs. Phillips added, beginning to look a little frazzled.

"Yes, was it you?" the lady asked, not looking up.

"No, we think she paged herself," I said.

"I see," the lady answered, and I wondered what she was thinking.

Since she said nothing more, I was just about to suggest that we check out all the snack bars when I heard the familiar shriek.

"Hyeeee!"

It was unmistakably Courtney. It was vintage Courtney. I turned around. As if she were on an African safari, Courtney led a single-file procession of about six boys, who were carrying her luggage on their heads and smiling, obviously dazzled. Courtney could do that to boys.

"Hi," she said to all of us who were gaping at her. She was carrying nothing but Wilheim Von Dog, her adorable white bichon frisé (pronounced "Bee-shawn Free-zay" with a slanty accent over the *e*). She was wearing a red plaid pleated skirt, white sweater, and matching plaid tam. A tiny purse hanging on a thin strap hung off her shoulder. It was very un-Courtney-like. She usually carried her money in her shoe or bra. In fact, she probably still did, and the purse was just for show. Wilheim Von Dog was dressed in the

13

same red plaid coat, little cap, and red sequined heart-shaped glasses to match Courtney's.

She introduced her line of boys so quickly that we immediately forgot their names. Larry, Sammy, Bobbie, and this is Gary, Barry, and Gerald.

"Courtney," I said after smiling at her new friends. "Remember how many times I told you about *my* friends Felicity and Dawn? Well, here they are."

Felicity and Dawn extended their hands. I just knew they were nervous. Courtney immediately produced a big sloppy kiss and a hug for everyone.

"Courtney, hungry?" my mom asked. "Because we can go out for something to eat."

I couldn't imagine Courtney not being hungry. But first she had to dismiss the luggage bearers.

"This is awesome," Felicity said as she watched the boys wave at Courtney while they backed away.

"Awesome," Dawn agreed. We went out of the airport with one of those little trucks with all of Courtney's luggage.

"I decided I didn't have fall or winter clothes, so I just bought everything new," Courtney was babbling.

She probably wouldn't unpack any of them. Courtney had an uncanny knack of pulling an outfit out of a suitcase as if she were performing.

"Courtney," Felicity said, running to keep up with her. I could see everyone in the airport turn their heads to look at Courtney. She was just so pretty.

"I was thinking," Felicity said, almost out of

breath. "What you need for your image is a publicity director. What about me?"

"Hmmmm," Courtney said as Dawn skipped beside her and piped, "And Courtney, how about a fan club? I was thinking of a theme song. We Love You, Courtney, to a catchy little tune. You could send everyone autographed pictures, and we could have T-shirts made up. It would be good for your image."

"Ummmm," Courtney said. Then, "Okay, super!"

I wondered what was going to happen when Courtney showed up at school as a full-fledged star.

# CHAPTER ═══
═══ THREE

She was much the same. Courtney attracted boys like walking flypaper. When she walked down the hall at I.S. 44 in her jeans and flaming orange top, about ten boys followed her.

"Hi, Courtney."

"Hi, Courtney."

"Hi, Courtney. How are you?"

"Hi, Courtney. How'd you like that test?"

"Oh, hi, Cath."

I was beginning to think of myself as Courtney's cousin Cathy. But I didn't want to stand out, and Courtney did it without trying.

Everything went perfectly that first week. I remember thinking if only I could have frozen it in time. The highlight was orchestra practice on Mondays and Thursdays after school. I could trust my cello. Actually, Courtney didn't come anywhere near blowing up the school. In fact, my mom was a little worried. She thought Courtney looked a little peaked and encouraged her to eat more. (Courtney—eat more!)

Also, Felicity and Dawn began to come around constantly. They set up headquarters in my bedroom. Felicity had a phone installed, and Dawn continually produced stacks of photographs for Courtney to autograph. Courtney was going to be a big star. She was becoming big business. Felicity was even trying to book her on a talk show.

"Excuse me," I said, trying to get to my desk. "I'll just be a minute. I need some books." See, asserting myself wasn't one of my strong suits. Anyone else might have yelled, "Get out! I have to do my homework!"

And where was Courtney all this time?

In the living room practicing for her part in the movie and saying the other parts in different voices. I still didn't see how she could act. There were all the lines to memorize and all the crying on cue. I know she never hid onions in her hands.

It was the last day of the first week of school, and I was marveling at how well everything was working out. I could study in the kitchen, and, though there was a lot of commotion in the apartment, I got a lot done.

Everything was fine. My mom had made one of my favorite dinners: meat loaf, mashed potatoes, gravy, and frozen peas. I didn't want to stare, but I couldn't help but notice Courtney. She had, well, weird eating habits. She had piled a mound of mashed potatoes in a soup spoon and carefully dotted it with green peas. Very quietly and without much fuss, she was sucking the peas out of the mashed potatoes as if she had a straw.

"It's good that you're eating more vegetables, Courtney, dear," my mom said.

"Have to keep up your strength," Howard added. I was proud of Howard. When my mom first met him, he wore only black ties and black suits, but now he had become colorful. He was wearing a white cable-knit sweater with red, white, and blue trim.

I guess I had been lulled into apathy when Courtney took us all by surprise.

"I need a detective," she said. A pea flew out of my mouth and landed in the butter dish.

"What's wrong, dear?" my mom asked, concerned.

"Maybe we can help?" Howard said, overlapping my mom.

Suddenly I had a queasy feeling in my stomach. I understood then that one normal week would be it. I wasn't sure what lay ahead, and I hated it when I lost control of who I thought I was.

18

But Courtney didn't usually announce getting into trouble. She just did it.

"No, no," Courtney said impatiently, tossing her coppery curls. I shut my eyes to get in touch with reality, then slowly opened them. It was just the dining room with my mom's white damask tablecloth, snowy cloth napkins, fresh-cut flowers in the middle of the table, and three people leaning in trying to figure out what one crazy almost-teenager was talking about.

"No, I need to buy a detective to hang out with, to learn from. See, I play the daughter of a detective in the movie."

The three of us sighed and leaned back.

"You could always watch a TV show," Howard said. "There are plenty of crime shows."

"Or we could get you a book," my mom said. (Hah! That was funny.)

"No, no, I need the real thing. Cathy, what are you doing tomorrow?"

"Nothing," I said in a high-pitched voice. There was no stopping Courtney when she got like this. I didn't know why I let her con me continually. You would think I'd get smarter as I got older. "Trust me," she always said. Well, anyway, I couldn't have her running around New York City alone.

"Don't worry, Cathy," she'd say. "That's your problem. You worry too much."

After dinner we went into the bedroom and lay

19

flat on our backs like beached whales. Out of the corner of my eye I could see Courtney pulling a long string of bubble gum out of her mouth and then cramming it back in. Pretty soon she'd get tired of that flavor and take another piece.

"There's a guy I like on the set. He's got midnight black curly hair and marble blue eyes. But we never get a chance to be alone."

"Uh-huh." I was still thinking of the other thing she had said. Hunting down a detective. Courtney had the attention span of a six-month infant.

She was also chewing double-time because she couldn't chew in school.

I had to finish up some homework and so did Courtney. She also had a ton of pictures to autograph. *I love you, too, Courtney* had become her signature. I looked over at her. She was using Wilheim Von Dog as a writing tablet, his little tongue hanging out and wagging from side to side.

Finally my mom stood in the doorway in her light blue robe. "Lights out, ladies."

I put my pencil in my red pencil case and placed my green ruler on my desk. I closed my blue binder with all the homework I had copied over in ink and then glanced over at my crazy cousin Courtney. She was slipping a little doggie nightgown on Wilheim Von Dog.

That night I experienced the kind of nightmare that wakes you up at four in the morning dazed and

20

in shock. Courtney and I were clinging together in front of a ten-foot-tall police officer on stilts. I didn't know where I was or even who I was when I woke up. Looking at the silvery moon casting a shadow in the room, I finally figured out who I was—Cathy Bushwick—and where I was—in our apartment at Central Park West and Eighty-third Street. We were right across from Central Park.

My nightmare was an omen.

Everything had been a reflection of my anxiety. Were we now going to start on one of our escapades and get in trouble? I felt I couldn't take it. Not now. Not during a school year. I had an invisible reputation to uphold.

"Courtney, are you asleep?"

"Uh-huh."

"Courtney, about this detective thing. I hope you're not thinking of anything that will get us into any trouble. First, there's your image to uphold, and second, there's my image to uphold. We could be the laughingstock of the whole school if anything goes wrong. Don't you think?"

"Uh-huh."

"Good, then we think alike. Now get some sleep."

I glanced over at Courtney. Her lacy eyelashes fanned out across her peaches-and-cream cheeks. Wilheim Von Dog slept with eyeshades on the opposite side of the pillow.

Courtney's perfect rosebud mouth that never needed lipstick or gloss formed the words *Uh-huh.*

21

Great.

Something had completely slipped my mind. Courtney talked in her sleep. She hadn't really heard a word I said. Or had she and she was pretending she hadn't?

# CHAPTER
## FOUR

The next morning Courtney was awake before I was. I poked the rumpled pink- and white-sprigged comforter to check to see if she was hiding under it. The sun was shining through the windows, and I could see it would be a beautiful Saturday.

Saturday!

I had planned to finish my algebra homework, practice my cello, and pick up the things from the cleaners because my mom was working at Phyllis's Zoo. She was the greatest animal agent in town— well, the only one anyway. Also, Felicity and Dawn would be coming at noon to set up their operations. I sighed. I like to concentrate on only one task at a time, and now I was forced to be like my cousin

Courtney—always in motion and doing four things at once. I put on my new designer jeans and a denim shirt and my brand-new sneaks and went into the kitchen to pour Cheerios with some milk into a bowl. Courtney had something elaborate planned. I could smell it.

She was sitting in a chair, innocently licking chunky peanut butter off an Oreo cookie. Oreos and peanut butter were her favorite breakfast. Mine, too, but I needed Cheerios now to steady my nerves.

"I found a detective agency," she said as easily as if she were saying, "I found a great fresh fruit store." Or "Look, I found a penny on the floor," or "I found another top in my trunk." She was wearing a flame red sweater with jeans. The sweater offset her orangey hair so that she looked more like a movie star than ever. Her green eyes were sparkling like rare gems.

"And?" I asked, aching to have an Oreo but feeling obligated to slosh through my Cheerios.

"They're located . . ." she said, taking a piece of paper out of her pocket. Great. While I was sleeping, she was looking up detective agencies.

"Okay, it's the Four A Detective Agency. The ad in the phone book said they're located right on the corner of Broadway and Forty-second Street. How do we get there?"

My spoon fell out of my hand. "Courtney, they've cleaned up the Times Square area a lot, but it's still no place for two almost-teenage girls to play on a Saturday."

It was as if she didn't hear me. She silently handed

me one pair of outsize sunglasses from the two she had picked up. Then I noticed that she was sitting on her trench coat.

"Relax, Cath, you have to relax more," she said as I bit into a Cheerio too hard and took a chunk out of my tongue.

"Get your raincoat, it looks like rain," she commanded. It was sunny out. She wanted us in disguise. I decided to humor her—once again.

I left the key under the welcome mat for Felicity and Dawn as we walked out of our apartment, then headed for the subway. Courtney loved the subways. Mainly because they were fast.

When we got on the C train, a man with a flute was playing a sparkling little tune and passing a cup. Courtney scribbled something down and passed it to him. I could tell he was a little disappointed.

"It's the name of my agent," she said in a low voice. "Tell her I said you should call."

We got out at Forty-second Street and walked over to Times Square. It was kind of quiet at nine-thirty in the morning.

"Courtney," I said, suddenly fearful. "Maybe we shouldn't do this. Can't you watch a detective on TV?"

"Trust me, Cathy. When I win an Academy Award, I'll include you in my list of thank-yous."

We located the old building. The doorman was too small for his uniform and had a hacking cough.

"We're here to see the Four A Detective Agency, please," Courtney said.

25

He paused to think about that for a while and then said, "Fifth floor, but the elevator's out. Watch the banister. Part of it fell off yesterday."

I shuddered. I wanted with all my heart to go home, but Courtney was stubborn. She had to play it out to the end, I knew.

After trudging up four flights of dusty steps, we were standing in front of Room 506. I looked down at Courtney's shoes. She was wearing her brand-new sneakers with the blinking red lights. Great. Talk about being subtle.

The windowpane on the door that said AAAA Detective Agency was frosted, bumpy glass you couldn't see through. One of the black A's was almost worn off.

"Maybe we should knock," Courtney whispered, as if someone were listening. On the other hand, there was no doorbell.

Courtney knocked timidly. No one answered. Then she knocked more loudly. No one answered. Then she knocked fiercely. No one answered.

Breathing a sigh of relief, I said, "Courtney, it looks like no one's in."

"No, I heard voices," she persisted. "It was when we were talking that they got quiet. There's someone in there. Trust me, Cath."

She was doing it to me again.

But I stopped her hand just as she was ready to reach for the credit card she kept in her sock. Courtney was very skilled at opening doors with plastic.

Come to think of it—why was she looking for a detective? She could teach them a few lessons.

Desperate, she tried the doorknob, which looked loose. I gasped as I looked at Courtney's hand. Oh, no, now what would we do.

She was holding the doorknob in her hand!

Just then the door opened. Courtney had been right. There *was* someone inside.

"Yes, how may I help you?"

We had to strain our necks to look up. There stood a really, really tall blond woman wearing one earring and chewing gum that I could smell. She had lipstick on her teeth.

"Is this the Four A Detective Agency?" Courtney asked boldly. I couldn't have said anything if my life depended on it.

"Who's the kid?" a voice said as we stepped inside. I took an immediate dislike to the voice, and a minute later I didn't like the man, either. He was short and squat with a pencil-thin mustache. The tall blond woman called him Myron. The furniture was green plastic and looked kind of slimy.

"Courtney," I said urgently, knowing it was wishful thinking. "Let's go home."

"Okay," she said. Now I knew we were really in trouble if Courtney agreed with me.

The tall blond woman looked us over and then moved to the door locking three bolts. I heard a clunk. That must have been the doorknob falling off. Courtney had tried to replace it. Well, we had finally done it, I thought. Now it was all over. These people were not nice. In fact, the whole building was not nice. I didn't see how Courtney was going to talk our way out of this.

"Who are you?" the tall blond woman asked.

"Who are you?" Courtney countered. Good thinking, Courtney, I thought.

"I asked you first," the woman said.

"I'm here to hire a detective," Courtney said with great authority. "For a job. I'll pay cash."

"How much?" the man with the skinny mustache asked.

"Whatever it takes," Courtney said. I put my hand over my eyes. This time Courtney had gone too far. The man and woman went into a huddle. For a second I thought they were going to do a folk dance. "Do you have parents?" the short man asked. Courtney piped up, "My name is Courtney Green, no *e* on the end, and I'm from Beverly, like the girl's name, Hills, California. I'm a movie star and I have parents, but they don't choose to be married to each other anymore. However, the split was friendly, and now I'm adjusted to it. He got the silver Rolls-Royce, and Joan, my mom, got the white one."

One thing about Courtney was that she didn't leave much to the imagination. That was basically how we got into trouble.

# CHAPTER FIVE

It occurred to me that they might want to kidnap us, and I wondered if they might change their minds about Courtney once they found out what she was really like. Maybe they would decide that no one would pay to have her back. All I knew was that I wanted to get out of the creepy green plastic office and that Courtney and I had made a whopper of a mistake.

But it was too late.

"Any more gum?" I heard Courtney say nervously. The tall blond lady was blowing bubbles now. She handed a piece to Courtney.

"Oh, Double Bubble. I haven't had this in years."

My eyeballs rolled to the ceiling, where I saw a

shred of paint dangling down. I knew that a lot of these old buildings on Times Square were headed for the wrecker's ball as they built up the area with new theaters and restaurants.

I was sure this had to be one of them. Why hadn't I thought of that before? Of course. All those boarded-up doors. This would be a perfect place to stage a kidnapping. No one would be able to find us. That's what I thought until I heard the knock on the door. It started out softly, then built to a fierce tapping and finally a fierce pounding. The tall blond lady strolled leisurely to the door. A man stood on the other side holding a doorknob.

"Police," he said. Another man was with him. "You're all under arrest."

"But how can you arrest detectives?" Courtney piped up.

"Who are you?" one of the police asked.

"Who are you?" Courtney replied. Well, they weren't dressed in uniform. I had to give Courtney credit. She had guts in a crisis.

"We asked you first," the other man said.

"Courtney Green, no *e* at the end, from Beverly, like the girl's name, Hills, California. I'm a movie star."

"Okay, Wynona Rider," one of the men said. "Come with us to Midtown South, where we'll fingerprint you."

I groaned inwardly.

"But we didn't do anything," Courtney pleaded. "I just came here to hire a detective."

"This is no detective agency. This is the home of the famous Bubble Gum Gang. We've been after them for a long time."

I noticed then that the short, squat man was also popping bubbles. He was using it as a distraction because as he popped one he took off for the door. He didn't count on Courtney and her superquick athletic reactions, though. As he passed her, she stuck her foot out—and down he went. She'd done it again—turned a situation around, and to her advantage.

The two men produced their police ID's as they helped the gang leader to his feet. "Detective Morrison, and this is my partner, Detective Kurtz. And these are notorious con artists who periodically try to sell the Brooklyn Bridge to tourists."

I wanted to make myself invisible and walk out of there. The building was wrecked. There was no such thing as a Four A Detective Agency, and Courtney and I were on our way to Midtown South, one precinct we had missed in our past travels and adventures.

I tapped one of the detectives on the shoulder. "Sir, we've *been* fingerprinted. I think at the Ninth Precinct." The dangly piece of paint fell from the ceiling and landed on his head.

"Look, I have two daughters," Detective Kurtz

31

said. "There are so many things to do in the City of
New York on a Saturday. There are museums. You
could ride bicycles. You could go to Central Park
and collect fall foliage." (Obviously one of his daughters wasn't named Courtney, I thought, but it was
apparent he didn't want to take us in.) "But instead
you have helped apprehend two criminals. I have to
ask you to accompany us to the precinct. Sorry, but
we have forms to fill out."

The detectives opened the desk drawers and found
that every drawer was filled with packets of money
wrapped in rubber bands. Bills were just stuffed
randomly in the drawers. I couldn't believe it.
These people were really crooks. We all trooped
down the steps, and a section of banister did fall
off. An omen of more bad luck to come? We arrived in the lobby and passed the doorman with
the hacking cough.

"Hi-ya, Nathan," Detective Morrison said. "How
ya' doin'?"

"Can't complain." And then he went back to his
coughing.

Times Square was still empty. It was still pretty
early. Times Square probably didn't wake up until
noon on a Saturday. We got in a purple car, and I
could sense immediately that Courtney was disappointed.

"I thought we could ride in one of those tur-

quoise and white cars with the siren screeching,"
she said.

I shut my eyes and kept them shut until we got to
Thirty-fifth Street between Eighth and Ninth ave-
nues. The two detectives sat in the front seat, and
Courtney and I were wedged between the two mem-
bers of the Bubble Gum Gang. We must have looked
like juvenile delinquents, and I hoped the press
would be kind.

Courtney and the tall blond lady popped their gum
at the same time and I jumped. When we went into
the precinct house, I noticed a pay phone to our left.

"Can I make a phone call?" Courtney asked
innocently.

I knew, I just knew, it wouldn't be to her parents,
Bernie and Joan, in Beverly Hills, California. It
wouldn't be to her agent, Mrs. Phillips. She would
want to call her director, Nigel Newman, who would
begin to spin the wheels of publicity that she thrived
on. No one knew Courtney like I knew Courtney.

There was a banner that proclaimed that Midtown
South was the busiest precinct in the world, and I
was afraid, with Courtney in it, it would get even
busier. There were vending machines with soft drinks
and snacks off to the side. They might come in handy
through the long, tedious day and night of paperwork
unless we could get someone to order out.

Courtney was sitting on a desk, swinging her legs.
Someone had given her a police hat, and she was
wearing it with the brim swung around to one side.

She was asking questions, and I could see she was doing the research she needed for her part.

Why hadn't we thought of New York's Finest before we got mixed up with the Bubble Gum Gang?

Then we sat in front of this very nice detective who thumped out our names and addresses on a rickety typewriter. Somehow I expected computers, but these detectives didn't have any. I think the city put all its money into vending machines.

Not long after I gave my mom's address and work phone number to the detective, I regretted it. I was still a minor. Did that mean they would interrupt her in the middle of an important booking? Say, the Flying Kazinskis, a juggling monkey act imported from Hungary. Or Howard. He had gone in to his office today, too. I wanted to fade into the tile on the walls, which I was studying. I wondered if my history teacher would like to know that the New York City Police Department started in 1845. I studied the plaques and clippings. Perhaps I could come back and do a report.

Mostly, I wanted to cry.

I heard Courtney giggling in the background. Everyone was making a fuss over her. Well, it was just because she was so pretty. Sometimes she looked like a toothpaste commercial. Or a sunscreen ad. She could advertise anything, and people would buy it.

Then I heard a deafening scream. It was Felicity and Dawn. Right behind them trooped the media, probably called by Nigel Newman. For after all, by accident or not, we had captured the notorious Bubble Gum Gang. I could hear one announcer saying, "These two little girls . . ." I groaned inwardly. They never let us grow up. We were always identified as two little girls.

Of course Courtney probably would never grow up. I wanted to slink through the door and walk away when a reporter approached me. I'm a very private person, and as she came closer, I had an electrifying thought. What if all the kids at school found out what we had been doing? What if they wrote it up for *Unplugged,* the school paper? We had never gotten into trouble in the fall—late August would have been stretching it.

Then I heard the only screech that mattered, and I shut my eyes. "My baby, my baby, are you all right?" I looked at my mom. One gold hoop earring was off. That was because she talked on the phone all the time. Right behind her came Howard, who was cracking up. Behind him waddled two pelicans. Yes, pelicans. Well I knew who was responsible for them, and obviously she didn't want to leave them in the car alone.

Howard took off his horn-rimmed glasses and wiped them with his tie. He found us funny.

I longed for my long braid. When we got into trouble in the past, I would just turn around so they would photograph my long braid. I felt I could almost hide behind it. Maybe I had had it cut off because I thought I wouldn't be getting into trouble anymore.

One of the police officers ordered pizza.

Yep, we had done it again. It was a regular three-ring circus.

# CHAPTER SIX

We got home just in time to see the news. Courtney flicked on the TV, and since I knew that she wasn't especially interested in current events, it was a clear guess what she was counting on.

If what she hoped came true, I would be dead of embarrassment by morning. I crossed and recrossed my fingers.

I lost.

When I heard the anchorman chuckle and say, "It seems two little girls from I.S. Forty-four in Manhattan captured a notorious band of crooks singlehandedly," I stuck my fingers in my ears and watched as he tried not to laugh out loud. Now everyone in school would know what we had done. News traveled fast.

Courtney was enjoying it thoroughly. She was smiling brightly. I felt like saying, "Look, Courtney, you don't have to get attention anymore, you're already signing more autographs than you have time for."

My mom shouted from the kitchen. "Courtney, phone for you!" I was pretty sure who that was.

"Uh-huh. Yeah, I will. No, I wasn't trying to get into trouble. Yeah. Uh-huh."

I knew who that was. Joan, her mother, was a fashion designer, and she kept the news on all day as she worked. She must have just gotten the word.

"You aren't mad at me, are you?"

That was one of Courtney's angelic tricks. I never for a minute believed it. But it melted everyone else's hearts. Besides, no one could ever stay mad at Courtney for long.

"Uh-huh, yeah. I'm a good guest. Uh-huh. I'll try. Okay. Uh-huh. No, I have enough bubble gum. Yeah, I love you, too."

She hung up and said, "That was Joan. She says hi."

Her family would always treat Courtney like a mischievous little girl.

"Joan has hired an acting coach for me," Courtney announced straight-faced. "She hopes the coach will keep me out of trouble. At least I won't have to hire any more detectives."

Courtney was reshooting a scene at an ice-cream parlor on West Ninety-sixth Street the next Saturday when the doorbell rang. I peered through the tiny peephole and saw a short woman who seemed just as wide as she was tall.

"Yoo-hoo, it's me!" she exclaimed.

I opened the door but kept the chain fastened.

"Natasha, dahlink, your acting coach, and you must be Courtney. Good cheekbones. We'll fix the hair, maybe get you a nice wig."

"But I'm not Courtney. I'm Cathy. My cousin Courtney will be home shortly. Won't you come in?"

"Can I trouble you for a little snack, dahlink? Unfortunately, I missed my lunch." I peered down into her tote bag and saw half a salami and a small jar of peanut butter.

After bringing her into the kitchen, I emptied the refrigerator to make Natasha a sandwich.

"Could I trouble you, please, for some ketchup and maybe a glass of that nice, bubbly milk?"

Just then Courtney appeared. She never warned you that she was there; she had a way of just materializing.

"You must be my acting coach," she said bluntly.

"You must be my little star," Natasha said, pleased, between bites. Natasha only coached child actors. They went into the living room to work, and the doorbell rang again. It was Felicity and Dawn. They marched into the bedroom, where they began to work.

I trailed after them and sat on the edge of one of my twin beds.

39

"Oh, careful, Cathy, those are freshly autographed pictures. Courtney likes to do them with a Pentel. They'll smear," Dawn said.

I jumped up as if I were sitting on hot coals.

"Whoops," I said.

Felicity was trying to book Courtney on a talk show called "Teens Who Made It and Their Lifestyles." Wilheim Von Dog was yipping at me as if I were an intruder. I looked longingly at my cello in the closet. But where could I practice? What I needed was to find a place to do my homework.

Suddenly I had an inspiration. It was an almost balmy early fall day. Why not go out onto the fire escape and do my homework there?

"I'll be on the fire escape if anyone wants to reach me," I announced to Felicity and Dawn. They nodded absentmindedly, but I wasn't sure they had heard me.

Felicity was absorbed. She wanted to be a public relations executive, just like her mom, when she graduated from college, and she thought this would look great on her résumé. Dawn didn't know what she wanted to be. She just wanted to have fun. Me, I wanted to be a writer when I grew up.

I went into the living room quietly so I didn't interrupt Courtney and Natasha.

"Now, dahlink, I want you to imagine you are a tree. Tell me everything you feel as a tree in the forest. One, two, three, go." She was reaching for her little jar of peanut butter.

40

"I'm going out to the fire escape," I said stiffly.

Courtney was deep in concentration. She could do that. She was a tree.

Finally I gathered my blue binder with the dividers from the vestibule where I had dropped it. My shiny green ruler was right beside it. I marched down the hall and opened the door leading to the fire escape.

I had never done anything like this before, and that left me feeling slightly unsettled. Courtney would have treated this as an adventure. But I couldn't. I felt as if nobody wanted me around. Or worse, no one even noticed I was around.

The hall door to the fire escape creaked open and the door slammed shut behind me. Finally, though, blessed peace and quiet. I was all alone. I could work on my algebra problems. I had everything I needed. Courtney was a tree. Felicity and Dawn were working on promoting her. I had no one to worry about.

I opened my blue binder. My three-hole red plastic pencil case was clipped right inside so I would never lose it. I had shopped in every drugstore for that particular kind. I unzipped it and reached inside for a pencil. It was empty.

I couldn't do my algebra. Then I remembered I left my pencils on my desk in algebra class. That was so unlike me.

Well, I had zillions of pencils in my desk at home. It would take a minute or two to get some. I stood

41

up, careful not to look down the four flights or not to look up through the trees.

The door was stuck. I tugged and pulled, but it wouldn't open. It was really frustrating. Like someone had lined it with glue. One really big tug and I could throw myself off the fire escape and into the courtyard below.

Then I realized something.

The fire escape door wasn't stuck.

It was locked.

I was locked out on the fire escape!

# CHAPTER SEVEN

**M**y first thought was that if I knocked on the door as loudly as I could, someone would rush to my rescue. I was obviously wrong. They were probably still exactly where I had left them: Felicity and Dawn babbling in my bedroom; Courtney and Natasha absorbed in being trees in the living room; and Wilheim Von Dog jumping around, yipping in staccato fashion because he wasn't getting any attention.

I was stuck.

Looking down, I caught my breath. There were three flights down to the second floor, and then a big leap to the ground. I didn't want to make that leap.

There was a dog on a chain strolling around the courtyard.

"Hi, pooch!" I yelled. No answer. He didn't even look up. If I could just have gotten him to bark, maybe someone would have come out to tell him to shut up and I could have yelled down to be saved.

To the right of me if I edged carefully along was an open window. A radio was playing music. Great. Mrs. Seltzer was home. She baked noodle pudding for all the neighbors. Help was on the way. All I had to do was get her attention. I couldn't believe I was in my own escapade without Courtney! I was the bad one now.

But it wasn't Mrs. Seltzer vacuuming. It was her cleaning person, and the minute the woman saw me in the window she screamed, left the room, and came back with a big pot. I slid back on the fire escape and pressed my back against the wall like those people they plead with not to jump off buildings.

Now I was really stuck.

How could I be crazier than my crazy cousin Courtney? What would she do in a situation like this? First of all, she never would have gotten herself into it. It was too boring. Courtney needed something more melodramatic. Something with a twist ending and a good headline to it. I wondered how long it would be before I was discovered by 911. Three years? I imagined the headlines: GIRL FOUND SPOUTING ALGEBRA PROBLEMS ON RUSTING FIRE ESCAPE. And the ugly rest of it. GIRL FALLS BEHIND HER CLASS BECAUSE SHE HAD THE WRONG ANSWERS. LIVED

FOR THREE YEARS ON ACORNS, APPLES FROM A TREE, AND SNOWFLAKES.

I began to panic.

It's never good to panic in a crisis. You can't think clearly, and I prided myself on thinking clearly. Clearly, I had to be discovered.

If I could just climb up one flight to the sixth floor, that might be easier than going down and getting dizzy. Old Mr. Winslow lived above Mrs. Seltzer. Maybe he could help me.

I forgot he was hard of hearing. I tapped on the open window, and all I heard was a steady stream of *zzzzz's*. He had an awful case of snoring. The window was actually wide open. Would I be a common criminal if I opened it a little farther and sneaked in and walked to his door? Then I would be free. The only problem was old Mr. Winslow had a short memory. Sometimes he remembered me and sometimes he didn't. Since Courtney came to live with us, he thought there were two of me.

But if I didn't take advantage of the situation and Seize the Day, as my teacher said, then I would be the girl on the rusting fire escape living on acorns, apples from a tree, and snowflakes. They would be searching everywhere, and I would be right outside the window. What's worse, I hadn't brought my toothbrush. Well, who knew.

I decided to make a run for it. Opening the window silently, carefully, I threw one leg in and then gathered up the other. Old Mr. Winslow stopped

45

snoring and I froze. Then I heard the *zzzz's* again and realized he must have been catching his breath. Holding my own breath, sneakers gripped in my hand, praying he wouldn't wake up to find me creeping across his living room, I made it to the front door. The doorknob stuck a little, but I pulled it open and, almost in tears, arrived in the carpeted hall in my stocking feet. I heard him yell loudly, "Hello. Who's there?"

I stopped to catch my breath and then I ducked into the door marked STAIRS. I felt like a fugitive. Where was Courtney when I needed her?

After running down the stairs, almost in tears, to the fifth floor, I arrived in front of 5J, my apartment, and realized I didn't have my keys. I was forced to ring the doorbell.

I heard the peephole slide open and knew I was being studied very carefully. I had just never been on the other side of my own door. Then one bolt unlocked and a second bolt unlocked and I heard the chain lock slide over.

"Yes, who is it?"

Whoever it was was reluctant to let any more people in an already overcrowded apartment. For a moment I got confused. Maybe I hadn't rung the doorbell to 5J. I felt like an alien from another planet. I mean, I did live there, didn't I?

"Who are you, dahlink?"

"It's me, Cathy."

"Do we know a Cathy?" Natasha asked. I could

picture Courtney still being a tree or a flower, deep in concentration. At this rate I'd have to wait until spring when she blossomed.

Suddenly the door was thrown open so wide, it almost slammed into the wall. Courtney grabbed me in her arms.

"Cath, what is it? Do you have amnesia? Where were you? It's okay. You live here. See, even Wilheim Von Dog knows you."

I looked around, dazed.

I thought Wilheim Von Dog was barking fiercely at me as if I were a stranger. But I was glad Courtney was through with her acting exercises. Her concentration when she was acting was awesome. Too bad it didn't continue on to her homework. In fact, schoolwork was the only thing Courtney wasn't good at.

Then I remembered I left my books and green ruler outside on the fire escape. As soon as I recovered, I would have to go back and get them.

I became aware of the unmistakable smell of Cookie in the apartment, and I knew Courtney hadn't spent all of the past half hour acting. She liked to take one of those slice-and-bake tubes, preferably chocolate chip, and bake Cookie. She just sliced the whole tube in half and made two cookies. First, it saved time since her time was valuable. And second, it was outrageous and so was she.

She was eating a hunk of Cookie topped with her favorite flavor of the month, week, day, or hour. Butter pecan. It was a weird combination, but then everything Courtney ate was weird.

Natasha, who had also topped a chunk of Cookie with butter pecan ice cream, and Courtney went back into the living room to work some more. Courtney's current assignment was to show sorrow. I watched her burst into tears while licking butter pecan ice cream off her Cookie.

"Wonderful, dahlink, think of the most tragic thing you can think of."

I knew what Courtney would do. She would picture a dognapper sneaking around her spotlighted pool in Beverly Hills and dognapping Wilheim Von Dog for a hefty ransom. Courtney couldn't bear to be separated from the little white puff ball for even a moment. When I left the room, she was racked with sobs.

My mom got home just then, shy one earring, and introduced herself to Natasha. "Keep up the good work, Courtney," she said.

Courtney nodded and kept on weeping.

I went into my bedroom.

I went to sit down on my bed and got stopped by Dawn, who said frantically, "Oh, Cath, no, no, no. Don't sit there. You might smear the pictures."

I looked longingly at my cello resting neatly in the closet next to my new clothes. Practicing made me feel better. It soothed my nerves.

The phone rang and Felicity answered it. Felicity told us, jumping up and down, that Courtney had gotten a spot on a talk show! It was called "Famous Teens and How They Lead Normal Lives." I shut my eyes. I was ready to go back on the fire escape and rescue my books.

Courtney normal?

Not by a long shot. I felt as if I was having an identity crisis. I knew that I needed to go somewhere else. To a comfortable place that would never disappoint me. Where excessive noise was discouraged. Where nobody knew my name.

It wasn't too far away from our apartment. It was the St. Agnes branch of the library on Amsterdam Avenue and Eighty-first Street. I loved it there and now I loved it even more. Blissfully, blissfully quiet. If there was ever any unwanted noise, the people in the library would put their fingers over their mouths and hiss *"Shhhh."*

I loved to read biographies. There was a great collection of them in the young adult division on the first floor. You could read about Theodore Roosevelt, the president, or Clara Barton, the famous nurse, or Helen Keller, who did so many admirable things. Knowing I shouldn't be using this precious time alone to daydream and dither, I strolled over to the biography section and picked up a few. After I read a bit, I would get into my homework.

I stacked my biographies on the table and flipped through them. What would it have been like to have been Jeanne d'Arc or Abraham Lincoln or Eleanor Roosevelt? Did they know they were destined to be famous when they were my age? This was the first chunk of quiet time and space I had had in a long time, so it was hard to settle down and do my homework.

I continued daydreaming, thinking about orchestra. There was a boy who sat next to me. He was left-handed. I was right-handed. We were both in the cello section. I had a raging crush on him. In certain phrases of the music, it was inevitable that he, being left-handed and me being right-handed, would touch elbows. It was like being struck by lightning. I liked him so much. In fact, I knew all the music, and instead of marking the music for accents and phrases, I marked it for elbow touching.

The problem was I didn't know if he felt the same tingle, and I couldn't very well ask him. Boys are so complicated, and I'm a little shy. No, a lot shy. I was afraid to talk to him! I was tongue-tied.

Even more frustrating than that I couldn't even discuss this with my Boy Expert and Main Confidante because she was busy working on *Chocolate Ice Cream* or sitting in the living room crying with Natasha and eating ice cream. The only part of her world she had let me into was that she liked a boy on the set. A real live movie star. She said he wasn't really interested in her, which was so un-Courtney-like. Every boy was interested in Courtney. Maybe that was why he fascinated her. How could a boy not like her?

I did my algebra homework first because that was

hardest. Then I wrote an English essay on what I wanted to be when I grew up. That was easy. A writer. Then I opened one of the biographies stacked on my desk. Queen Elizabeth II as a young woman. So much responsibility. I looked at the pictures of her coronation in 1952.

"Mind if I sit down?" a voice asked.

I looked up into enormous root-beer brown eyes and long, inky lashes. His complexion was ruddy and his smile made me want to smile. There was a cute pair of black wire-rimmed glasses slipping down his nose. "Sure," I said.

"Have you read all these bios?" he asked, picking one up. "I love history. It's my favorite subject. I wish I had more time to read."

"I know what you mean."

I thought about my hectic homelife. There was no way of explaining that three-ring circus to an ordinary kid like this. My mom had shipped the pelicans back to Florida and was currently grooming Daisy, a rambunctious chimpanzee, for a role in a kid movie. No one would believe it. My house was just too showbizzy for words. I would feel uncomfortable if this nice boy even knew the truth about me.

"Do you come here often?" he asked.

I nodded. "It's a good place to study."

He nodded, too. I thought it was funny that there were some guys you could talk to and others you couldn't. Of course, I still really liked the boy in orchestra.

51

"My name is Zachary. What's yours?"

"Cathy. Cathy Bushwick." I glanced at my Timex watch. It was after five. I liked to help my mom make dinner because she worked so hard. The past week she had been trying to make a deal for a rhino named Rory.

"I have to go now. Nice meeting you," I said. I sincerely hoped that Natasha hadn't made little sandwiches out of dinner.

"Okay, see you around," he said, opening up a book.

I glanced at him, and then it hit me how cute he was. But I was loyal to the boy in orchestra. I knew I couldn't like more than one boy at a time, though I was sure Courtney could. As I walked out of the library, I understood how I needed things to be black and white—and not gray.

I wished that I could find some quality time with Courtney to discuss the "boy department," as my mom called it. Courtney was so sophisticated when it came to boys. She would know exactly how to handle the boy in orchestra—and maybe even Zachary.

# CHAPTER EIGHT

I went back to the library time after time to study, but never saw Zach. Maybe his family had moved to Idaho. Sometimes I would think I saw him with his wire-rimmed glasses slipping down his nose, but it always turned out to be someone else.

One day after school I sat stroking Wilheim Von Dog and watching Natasha and Courtney in the living room. Natasha was coaching Courtney on what to say on the talk show "Famous Teens and How They Lead Normal Lives." She was emphasizing her point with a ham on rye.

"Dahlink," she said to Courtney, who was sitting on the couch hanging on to every word her acting coach said. "Ze trick to being on a talk show is to never, ever reveal the truth. Not even one kernel of it."

She took a bite out of her ham sandwich.

"But that wouldn't be honest," I butted in.

"Yes, yes, true. But Courtney must have ze mystery. No one should really know what she's thinking, what she's up to."

I really couldn't get used to Courtney being a movie star. Not the Courtney I knew, the one who would spill her guts at the drop of a hat.

Felicity and Dawn came into the living room. Felicity was beaming at her little star friend. Dawn was smiling, too. I knew how they felt. I had recently mastered a Mozart piece on the cello, the one where I bumped elbows with Wally (that's his name) sixteen times. I was feeling proud of myself, too.

Maybe after the talk show Courtney and I could have a heart-to-heart about boys. I could have used some help with Wally, and I knew boys were never very far from her mind no matter how involved she was with her work. Just because she was a star in *Chocolate Ice Cream* didn't mean she didn't melt at the sight of the blue eyes of her co-star, Josh.

On the next Saturday, the day of the talk show, I got up early and saw Courtney had, surprisingly, gotten up even earlier. She was sitting in front of the mirror on the vanity table making gross faces. She was doing the voice exercises Natasha had given her. Anyone else would have looked like the Creature from the Black Lagoon, but Courtney still was pretty. She was really taking her career seriously. I loved the sound of that. It might mean a trouble-free Courtney.

After breakfast, which consisted of Cheerios and a banana for me and two tablespoons of chunky peanut butter smeared on three Oreo cookies for Courtney, we were off.

All of us met downstairs and piled into two cabs. Felicity and Dawn stuffed their promotional material into one. I, Natasha, Courtney, in her heart-shaped red-sequined sunglasses with Wilheim Von Dog in his little matching pair, took the other one. I was squished in the middle as Natasha quizzed Courtney on questions she might be asked.

"Now, dahlink, what do you say if someone asks if you can still have a normal homelife despite the fact that you are a big movie star?"

I thought about that.

What was the definition of *normal?*

That was when I began to have a funny, queasy premonition about this talk show.

"I'm as normal as blueberry pie," Courtney answered. She sounded like Courtney imitating someone else. I couldn't quite put my finger on it. She sounded like Courtney imitating Natasha imitating Courtney. What could go wrong? Nothing could go wrong. I even asked Howard to program our VCR to record the event. Therefore I must be confident. Nothing could happen. What could go wrong? I found myself staring at the doughnut in Natasha's hand.

Felicity and Dawn's cab passed us and we waved. We got out in front of Rockefeller Center where the studios were located in the NBC building. I was impressed.

Courtney was becoming a big-time star, but she was my cousin and I knew her first. I also knew the real Courtney, the one who could turn any event around to become an adventure.

Courtney was wearing a fuzzy white angora sweater with puffy sleeves and a green- and blue-plaid pleated skirt, fringed at the hem. She wore thick socks and penny loafers. Felicity and Dawn had selected her clothes so she looked like a fantasy thirteen-year-old from a Disney movie. She was anything but, so I thought it was a pretty clever disguise. Wilheim Von Dog wore a little blue and green jumper over his sparkling white fur. With his tiny sunglasses he looked like a movie star, too.

I felt a little in awe as we were ushered around the sound stage. We saw the room where the director sat and the many little cameras that showed the program in progress. To think that my crazy cousin Courtney would be viewed at so many angles while we watched from out front was very interesting. The experience should make a good paper for school.

On the stage were five straight-backed chairs arranged in a semicircle. We all knew who was going to be on the show with Courtney: a champion gymnast; an almost Olympic figure skater; a ballerina; a girl who trained Arabian horses; and Courtney, a real live movie star soon to be appearing in the feel-good romantic comedy *Chocolate Ice Cream,* guaranteed to melt everyone's heart.

They sat all the girls on the stage. Courtney was smiling as if she were auditioning for a toothpaste commercial. I would have even been too shy to sit in the group. My knees knocked together every time I read a paper out loud in English class.

The talk show was called "Roberta's Hour," but it only lasted for a half hour so maybe they should have called it "Roberta's Half Hour." All the guests had been booked a long time in advance except for Courtney, who was scheduled because someone had backed out of their engagement.

I could see that Wilheim Von Dog's tongue was out. He was sitting in Courtney's lap, panting. Maybe the hot lights were too much for him. Maybe he needed a drink. Maybe Courtney shouldn't have brought him with her, but then I knew that he acted as her security blanket. She could hide behind him, something she'd never let on she was doing. Courtney could be very tricky.

A woman from the audience walked up to the microphone near the stage. "How old were you when you started to go to parties?" she asked the figure skater.

The cameras zoomed in on the ice-skating champ, who was wearing a short skirt and had very muscular legs. She answered a little defensively, I thought, and I found myself praying that Courtney would do better. "I've been skating since I was three. My dad is my coach, and I've never missed a birthday party. In fact, I have a lot of friends."

A hand shot up. Everyone turned as Roberta called on a young man who stepped up to the microphone. "I'd like to ask a question of the movie star." I shut my eyes and crossed my fingers. "Do you consider yourself normal? Do you go to school? Have you ever been on that TV show 'Extra'?"

Courtney blinked. Had she succumbed to stage fright? I wondered. Oh, no, I couldn't believe it. Courtney popped something into her mouth without looking. It was bubble gum, but she didn't check out the flavor first. It was Love that Licorice. The flavor that blackened your teeth and made the inside of your mouth look like the inside of a cave. Now she was stuck. She couldn't reach in and take it out. I guess she could swallow it.

"Dahlink," she said, but it was a little hard to hear her. "I'm as normal as blueberry pie." And then she flashed a picture-perfect Courtney smile, only this time her teeth were all black.

The scream came from the audience, and I didn't realize what had happened at first. In that second between shock and discovery I heard someone yell, "Stop that dog!"

Then I heard, "Stop that girl!"

Then I connected it. Wilheim Von Dog had made

58

a mad dash off Courtney's lap and was running out of Studio D.

After scampering among the snakelike cables and the imposing cameras, he had bolted out of the studio. Unfortunately, he landed in another set. I was familiar with it because my mom sometimes watched the show when she had time. It was a cooking show, and it was called "Betty's Kitchen, Where Anything Can Happen."

"Wilheim Von Dog!" Courtney screamed as she left the set running after him. I watched the camera move back, and checked a TV monitor that showed one-sixteenth of Courtney's chair and the other girls.

Then quickly Felicity, Dawn, Natasha, and I ran into the audience of the set on Studio C. I watched Courtney crash into Betty, a tall lady who looked as if she was wearing a chestnut-colored wig. She dropped an artichoke heart on the floor she was so surprised. For a second I didn't see Wilheim Von Dog and if I couldn't see him, Courtney couldn't see him, and I knew she never went anywhere without that dog.

Then I remembered something even more unsettling.

Wilheim Von Dog got fed table scraps. One thing I knew he really enjoyed were artichoke hearts.

# CHAPTER NINE

Courtney got to the kitchen set in seconds to save her poor dog who, by the way, was having a wonderful time. Betty was so nervous she now dropped a soup bone on the floor. Wilheim Von Dog was chasing it around the floor under the table. Courtney tackled Wilheim not to protect Betty's Kitchen but to protect her dog. For Courtney, Wilheim Von Dog came first. Absolutely. They were devoted to each other. The only trouble was me. I didn't see Courtney in time as I jumped up on the stage, oblivious to the cameras, and plopped down on top of Wilheim Von Dog. Now there were the two of us rolling on the floor with poor Wilheim Von Dog squeaking and yipping. Some of the camera people were laughing, and I realized we had done it again. Even though I wasn't sure exactly what we had done, yet.

Betty was saying in a high, almost falsetto voice, "If you don't have a soup bone, then use, well, canned broth should do. Meat is too high in fat."

Courtney and I got up off the floor.

"Who are you?" she asked.

"I'm Courtney Green, no *e* at the end, and I'm from Beverly, like the girl's name, Hills, California." Just then Wilheim Von Dog gave a great leap and scampered out of her arms and on to the long, wooden table, dragging the soup bone with him. I squeezed my eyes shut, as if that could ward off the pain of embarrassment and humiliation. But I could see the audience out of the corner of my eye. Maybe some of the audience of "Famous Teens" had followed us into "Betty's Kitchen, Where Anything Can Happen." I saw the cameras and they were focused like one giant eye on Courtney and me and the quivering Wilheim Von Dog, who refused to be parted from his soup bone.

Betty needed onions sliced, and since she was a good sport she had decided to incorporate us into her show. She asked Courtney to slice the onions. Oh, no, I thought. Courtney wasn't very handy. If she didn't lose a finger, we'd all be lucky.

Now we were on national television in the world-famous studios of NBC. Courtney snitched an onion slice. You couldn't keep food out of her mouth for long. Wilheim Von Dog had nicely cleaned his soup bone, and Betty was shelling beans.

"The pièce de résistance on your vegetable platter will be string beans sautéed with onions."

She handed another onion to Courtney to begin peeling, and I could tell that Courtney was near flooding the place with tears from the first onion. That's one thing you never see my crazy cousin Courtney do. Cry. Life was always too much fun, but onions could bring down even Courtney.

The reason Betty didn't give me a job was that I had my back to the audience. I was hoping to blend in with the appliances.

"Our bread, the staff of life, has been baking to a golden, crispy brown. Can you take it out, uh, dear?"

"Do you have any peanut butter?" I heard Courtney ask, and I almost slithered down the refrigerator. I could see that this lady, Betty, of "Betty's Kitchen, Where Anything Can Happen," was a very smart lady. If she had called security and had Courtney, me, and Courtney's dog removed, it would not have been good for public relations. Besides, all her viewers would have seen her do it.

This way she might actually gain viewers because Courtney was a movie star in the making. Of course, Courtney might lose some of her own audience.

Courtney sampled some warm bread and passed a tidbit down to Wilheim Von Dog. Betty was waiting apprehensively for Courtney's approval. Courtney gave her a thumbs-up. I couldn't have been happier.

I spotted Felicity and Dawn standing with their hands over their faces, shaking their heads. In five minutes or less Courtney had undone all the work everyone had done in building her positive, wholesome image.

Natasha was smiling. But it was hard to tell if she was enjoying this new turn of events or liked the food show because she could pick up some new recipes.

Oh, well, I thought. The worst is over. Nothing can happen now. We've done all of the meal. Not quite, I learned.

"And now for dessert. Rich, velvety chocolate cake with fudgy frosting said to have been served at the court of the king of France in the seventeenth century."

"Then how did you get it?" Courtney blurted out, and I heard an audible sigh. I realized I was the one sighing. I almost passed out, I wanted to get out of there so bad.

Betty handed Courtney a potholder, and Courtney managed to take the cake out of the oven without dropping it.

"Before ladeling this rich and thick frosting," Betty was saying, "let it cool. Then drizzle it like the spring rain onto your cake. But be careful not to dip your thumb into it too many times, or you won't have enough frosting for your cake." She stopped to laugh at her own joke.

No one really saw Wilheim Von Dog advance to the pan of cooling frosting. He settled below it like a cat on a hearth. Courtney caught on to what he was doing first and rushed to get him. So did I a second later, and again, Courtney and I landed in a heap on the floor with Wilheim Von Dog under us.

And then an unfortunate incident happened.

Betty ran to save the pot of frosting and accidentally bumped the handle, nudging the pot onto its side so the frosting drizzled like spring rain onto Wilheim Von Dog. As it turned out, the two became one. I looked at the floor expecting a big chocolate puddle, but it wasn't there. Mostly the frosting got all over Wilheim Von Dog. We now had a chocolate dog. Courtney picked him up and cuddled him close to her. The whole audience as well as the crew burst out laughing as Wilheim Von Dog licked himself like a cat. I could hear noise in the director's booth. They were cracking up. Great. I could see it now. GIRL WITH CHOCOLATE DOG. Or worse, MOVIE STAR'S DOG SWEET ON CHOCOLATE. The publicity angles were endless. Maybe her director, Nigel Newman, would like this because it would help to publicize the movie.

"Of course the cake doesn't really need double chocolate fudgy frosting. You can always spritz a little whipped cream and some fresh peach slices on it. That will do just as well, and it's much better for you," Betty was saying. I could see she was getting a little more flustered.

Wilheim Von Dog would need to be de-chocolatized in our tub. It might be hard to evacuate Daisy, the very smart chimp who had taken up headquarters behind the shower curtain in our bathtub. My mom was chimp-sitting until the trainer got back from safari.

I could see poor Betty looking for some kind of cue that the show was over. She really wanted it to be, and I couldn't blame her. I watched a young man stretching his hands as if he had gum in them. The clock on the wall showed there were five minutes to go. Betty's chocolate sauce was gone, vanished. Two almost-teen girls had destroyed her program. I felt sadder and sadder. I wanted to say something to Betty, but I knew somehow it would be better not to. It would be kinder if we just quietly disappeared from her life.

"This has been 'Betty's Kitchen, Where Anything Can Happen,' " she said. She looked at the two of us, almost for approval. "Tune in tomorrow when we'll bake Tuna Supreme with baby carrots and Bombay celery, all recipes from the crowned heads of Europe."

Right before the director yelled "Cut," Courtney said, "I bet they ate better than that."

When the show was finally over, poor Betty wiped her forehead with her apron. She picked up her soup bone and, head held high, walked off the set to her dressing room.

Courtney and I left with Wilheim Von Dog still licking himself like a cat.

# CHAPTER TEN

We survived "Betty's Kitchen, Where Anything Can Happen." Of course, we didn't escape publicity entirely. The news showed a piece on the little chocolate-covered dog and Courtney the movie star from *Chocolate Ice Cream.* Then *Unplugged,* our school newspaper, did an article on Courtney because we never had a movie star in our midst. It was suggested by Felicity and Dawn.

"It will be good for her image," Felicity said. Dawn nodded.

As far as I was concerned, Courtney's image needed more than a little work.

Courtney pronounced everything "super." She said they didn't have a school newspaper in her junior high school in Beverly Hills. I assured her they did, but she had probably never read it.

Natasha continued to hold court. Mostly in the kitchen.

I mentioned to my mom that Natasha had a really healthy appetite, and my mom said, "She's our guest. What's a little bologna? When you visit Courtney in Beverly Hills, you're her guest."

Life, surprisingly, fell into place, meaning it was orderly. Only one thing was making me slightly anxious. The orchestra was practicing for a recital to be held in afternoon assembly on Friday. I felt as if I had a vibrating elbow, I had touched Wally so much.

Once he looked up from his music and smiled at me. I almost dropped my bow. Then I lost my place because I was trying to decide if he really smiled at me or if something funny ran through his mind. It felt as if I were photographing his every move and gesture so I could paste them in a scrapbook when I got home. But I never got up the nerve to really talk to him. I was speechless.

I also didn't know if he felt the same shot of electricity when our elbows touched. Was his elbow vibrating? I only knew I really liked him. I was madly in like with him, and if I didn't tell someone, I would burst.

My biggest fear was that Mr. Korda would yell at me for making a mistake because I acted like such a blithering idiot around this boy. Oh, it wasn't that

Wally was so heartbreakingly handsome. He wasn't. He wasn't the best-looking boy in the school by far. He had blond hair that fell in his eyes so that he had to brush it away. I would gladly have done that for him. He had hazel eyes, and his complexion was pink like peach pie. I liked to watch his hands out of the corner of my eye. He had long, tapering fingers. I knew he was sensitive because boys didn't usually choose to play the cello. Maybe he would go to the Juilliard School of Music. Me, I knew I wasn't good enough.

Everyone called him Wally, but the teachers called him Walter. Walter Osterman. He was also in my history class. I found it hard to concentrate there, also, and history was one of my favorite subjects.

Thursday night before the recital Courtney and I were alone in our room. Felicity and Dawn had left hours ago. Natasha had taken a peanut butter and jelly hero home for her dinner. My mom was in the kitchen making chicken pot pies. Daisy was chattering in the shower. It almost sounded like "The Star-Spangled Banner." Howard was in the front room reading the paper.

It was just us.

"Courtney, there's this boy . . ." I began.

"Oh, I know, he's driving me crazy. Absolutely crazy."

"Who?" I said, sitting up on my elbows.

"Josh. He doesn't even know I'm alive even when

68

we kiss." Suddenly I became terribly interested. "You kiss a guy?"

"Well, yeah, sure. It's in the script, but I can tell he's thinking about something else."

"Someone else?"

"I don't think so. Maybe he's thinking about a nice, drooly slice of pizza."

"You're kidding. Well, what are you thinking about?"

"Him," she said, popping a bubble.

"Wow, you really like this boy," I said. That was a little un-Courtney-like. She usually didn't care very much.

She turned over on her stomach and popped her gum so hard I thought there was a thunderclap. "But he doesn't know I exist. It's really hard to concentrate when you like someone that much. Know what I mean?"

Then I remembered that I had started the conversation and that I was the one who needed some help with my crush on Wally. But it was too late.

"Dinner's ready, everybody!" my mom yelled from the kitchen. I never understood how my mom juggled everything, but I wanted to be just like her when I grew up. She ran the most successful animal talent agency in New York City (well, it was the only one), ran a household, and still had time for all of us.

The best thing about her was that I could tell her anything. As I was selecting a bottle of salad dressing and drizzling it on my salad, I decided to tell my

69

mom about Wally. After dinner. She would know what to do. She was smart, and she knew a lot of things because she had been my age once.

Courtney had spread a spoonful of chicken pot pie on a piece of rye bread and was now covering it with salad dressing. She smiled at me. Her weird eating habits had gotten even weirder. She would probably request seconds on everything, I knew, including dessert, which turned out to be velvety rich chocolate cake with double rich, double chocolate fudgy frosting. My mom had jotted down the recipe during that crazy show.

"So, the big recital is coming up," Howard said.

"Uh-huh," I said, nervous just thinking about it. Sometimes I dreamed of Wally's and my elbows being glued together when we played the Bach piece or the Mozart thing.

"I'm sorry I can't get off work to come," Howard said.

"I'll be there," Courtney announced, making another rye-bread-and-chicken-pot-pie sandwich. She had to be, of course.

"I'll be there," my mom said, smiling.

Great. I'll be so nervous, I'll probably drop my bow, bend over to pick it up, and bump into Wally's knee, knocking out a tooth.

Maybe I should tell Mom to stay home. Something was bound to go wrong. I watched Courtney go excavating for the tiny chunks of chicken in the chicken pot pie and placing them on her knife when she found them.

"Mom, can I help with the dishes after dinner?" I pleaded.

"How can I say no to that, Cathy, dear, but it's a lot easier with the dishwasher."

Howard had bought us a lot of things. We moved into a new co-op apartment. I got ice-skating lessons, and even got a trip to Beverly Hills to visit Courtney. I had all my California photos pasted in my scrapbook, which I had painstakingly lettered with multicolor Pentels. Well, that's just the way I am.

My mom served the cake, coffee for her and Howard, and big bubbly glasses of white chilled milk for Courtney and me.

"Super," squealed Courtney. It was like living with a seven-year-old.

"Sure, Cath," my mom said, answering my question about helping with the dishes, and I knew she caught my jist. I had a problem, and I needed to talk it over with her.

After dinner Howard took his calculator and accountantlike pens into the little study, and Courtney went into the living room with her script. It sounded as if she was talking to herself, but she was just going over her lines.

"So, Cathy, how is everything in the Boy Department," my mom said. Talk about a mind reader.

"Well, there's this guy I like a lot. He sits next to me in orchestra, but, well, we've never spoken, not

71

really. Not beyond checking to see what page we're on."

I could hear Courtney in the front room say nice and loud, "The only boy I've been close to is my brother."

"I feel close to this boy, though we don't talk," I confessed.

"But you don't know him, dear," my mom said.

"It seems as if I've known you all my life," we heard Courtney say from the living room, rehearsing. I heard a loud pop, and I knew she was chewing an after-dinner wad of gourmet bubble gum.

"It sounds as if you have a good old-fashioned crush," my mom said. "These things come and go. I logged about eighty-seven when I was your age. You should get to know him as a friend, Cath."

"Yes, but." How could I disagree with my own mom? I knew I liked Wally more than any boy I had ever met. The trouble was I felt very uncomfortable around him.

I was shy.

And I could sense that Wally was shy.

That night, when the lights were out and Courtney and I were in bed, I hesitated to say anything because her time was valuable and she needed her sleep. The one thing that threw me off was that she chewed bubble gum while she was sleeping, so I couldn't tell if she was awake or not.

Also, she was known to talk in her sleep.

"Courtney, are you asleep?"

"Uh-huh."

"There's this boy I like, Wally. He plays cello right next to me in orchestra. What should I do?"

"Do?" Courtney said.

I waited for more, but there was no more. Soon the gum cracking stopped, and I realized Courtney really was asleep. I liked Wally and still didn't know what to do about it.

# CHAPTER ELEVEN

The recital the last period of the day went without a hitch except during the Tchaikovsky piece when I almost dropped a sheet of music because I wasn't really concentrating. I was daydreaming about a date with Wally. We went to an ice-cream shop on Broadway, and we had ice-cream sodas and talked and became friends as my mom had suggested. I still hadn't said much of anything to Wally. Sometimes it felt as if I had a glob of peanut butter stuck to the roof of my mouth with no milk in sight. I noticed out of the corner of my eye that he almost dropped his music as well. I wondered if he liked me, too. Did his elbow tingle? I just didn't know. That's how it was with crushes. We touched elbows eleven times, and I found myself waiting for each new passage.

My mom and Courtney came backstage to meet me afterward. Wally had disappeared with what was probably his family.

Staring at Courtney, I found it hard to believe she liked only one boy right now. My mind flashed on the boy I had met briefly in the library. I didn't have a crush on him, but I could talk to him easily.

"How about some ice cream, girls?" my mom said, snapping my picture with an Instamatic camera. I hated to have my picture taken. Courtney loved it.

We went to the same ice-cream shop on Broadway that had been in my Wally daydream. I had my favorite flavor, vanilla. Courtney had one of her usual concoctions. Pumpkin, mint chocolate chip, and peanut butter cup topped with a dollop of fresh whipped cream, crushed nuts, and a juicy cherry.

"How would you like to come on a shoot with Jolly the giraffe tomorrow?" my mom asked. "We're shooting a truck commercial. Jolly's going to run alongside it."

Courtney looked up from her super-deluxe combination. "Oh, I love giraffes," she squeaked. "They're so graceful. They look like upside-down question marks and move like you learn in modern dance. Run, run, run, run—leap."

"Well," my mom said. "I thought I'd pack some egg-salad sandwiches."

Those were my favorite. My mom made them with a dash of cayenne pepper and paper-thin slices of cucumber. No one's egg salad was like hers.

"We'll get up early and ride to the location in the truck with the trainer. Jolly will be in the back," she said.

"Yea!" Courtney said in one loud outburst. Everyone turned around. Well, it was just that Courtney was so pretty and loved life so much.

"This will be a nice adventure for you, Courtney," my mom said. "We'll drive out to the wilds of New Jersey."

I closed my eyes and shuddered. I hoped my mom meant a supervised adventure. The last thing we needed with Courtney was something unexpected. It would be bad for her image, and Felicity and Dawn would have heart attacks before they graduated from junior high.

But I figured there was no way she could get into trouble on a wildlife set in New Jersey. What could she do? The director would keep her at a distance, and the egg-salad sandwiches would keep her entertained. My mom would make a lot, and Courtney could eat a lot.

Then, too, Jolly the giraffe couldn't be ruffled. He was an old pro. He had done a commercial for *National Geographic* magazine, and he had been in the movie *Letters from Africa.* As giraffes go, Jolly was a superstar.

76

"I've never seen a real giraffe before," Courtney cooed. I began to be suspicious. I guess it was something in the tone of her voice. "There are no zoos in California."

I exploded.

"Are, too," I said.

"Are not."

"Too."

"Not."

"Courtney, there's the very famous and spectacular San Diego Zoo for starters."

"Oh," she said, smiling. "Well, how would I know about zoos? I'm too busy with boys." At least she was honest.

The next day we were riding in the truck through New Jersey. I played a game with myself. I pretended the Great Swamp in Chatham was the wilds of Africa. I liked to test my imagination as a writer. I peered at Jolly the giraffe, who I had to admit did look awesome. My mom said he was nineteen feet tall and grazed in the treetops.

We stopped and had a picnic with cold milk and egg-salad sandwiches. There was also fresh fruit and cookies for dessert.

Courtney strolled over to the special trailer containing Jolly the giraffe and tapped the glass.

"Kootchy, kootchy, koo," she said, waving a cookie.

After several escapades with my crazy cousin Courtney, I had developed a sixth sense about what she was thinking. I had become an expert on ESP. But this time it wasn't working. I still couldn't see how she could get us into trouble. There was no way. It was ironclad. My mom was with us.

When we got to the location, the director, who was in tall leather boots and a jacket to match, screamed, "Cue the giraffe!" I thought it was very impressive.

Jolly, old pro that he was, stepped off the trailer on his almost pencil-thin legs, as gracefully as a ballet dancer, and looked down at us.

I could tell Courtney was thrilled.

"Cue the truck driver!" the director screamed through a megaphone. The camera people were carrying hand-held cameras because, I guess, you couldn't use the big ones in the high junglelike grass.

My job was to keep Courtney away from the cameras, and that wasn't too hard because, for once, she wasn't the center of attention.

Most of the animals my mom worked with got little treats for doing their jobs or performing their stunts. Marshmallows or gumdrops or big slabs of red meat. But everyone knew Jolly could find his own treats. Once out in the open he stretched his awesome nineteen-foot frame to shop among the treetops.

"Good boy," I could hear his trainer say.

I could hardly imagine a temperamental giraffe. That

78

would be like a rambunctious rhino or a moody elephant.

"Wow, this is just so super. I've never seen a commercial shot!" Courtney shouted.

"Courtney, you were in a movie!" I reminded her.

"I know. But not with a giraffe."

I studied my cousin Courtney. It was a hot, humid early fall day, and Courtney, who thought every day was summer, was wearing a wild pink midriff top. It went with her red-sequined heart-shaped sunglasses and offset her coppery curls.

I saw a little crowd forming near a clump of trees in the southwest corner of the shoot. One man was snapping pictures. Well, who wouldn't want a picture of a magnificent giraffe like Jolly?

My mom came over to us. "The director's cuing the truck driver now," she said. "The action should begin soon. We just have to coax Jolly away from the tree. Poor dear, he's been cooped up working the last few weeks."

"That doesn't seem fair," I said.

She shook her head. "No, Jolly is happy. That's how he got his name. Besides, he was in the San Diego Zoo before this, so he's freer now than he ever was."

"See," I said triumphantly, turning to Courtney. But there was an empty space where my cousin Courtney had been standing. It had happened so fast that the screaming didn't register.

The little crowd gathered in the southwest corner

79

went wild screaming, "Go, go, go!" as if they were at a sporting event.

Only one person in the world could inspire that kind of crazed response.

I thought I knew her, but this time she had gone to new heights. She was always springing new talents on me. Hidden accomplishments. This time she had sprinted up a tree faster than lightning. If tree climbing had been included in the Olympics, Courtney would represent the United States. But why, oh, why, I asked myself in that brief minute of horror, why had she done it?

As soon as I asked the question, I had my answer.

Jolly's trainer was trying to pull Jolly away from Courtney, who was at the top of the tree hanging on and hugging him.

Courtney may love animals, but this was going too far. She was now feeding Jolly clumps of leaves. It was love at first sight. Then, with a sinking sensation in my stomach, I noticed something: The people in the southwest corner had a lot of cameras, and they must be taking a lot of pictures. But this was Chatham, New Jersey. There was no way any of those pictures could find their way into the New York papers.

Could they?

I looked up and up and up at Courtney, who wasn't budging. Neither was Jolly. The fire department had been called, and after they arrived they ran around trying to find the best spot for a net in case Courtney fell or decided to jump. But common sense should have told everyone that if Courtney got up, she could get down.

It was Jolly the giraffe they had to worry about. His trainer couldn't pry him away from Courtney. They had fallen in love.

# CHAPTER ━━━━
━━━━ TWELVE

The fire department had decided to scale the tree and pry Jolly away from Courtney. Why they just didn't ask Courtney to come down I'll never know. They probably thought she was scared and couldn't move. Little did they guess she was having the time of her life and could have been down to the ground in about three seconds flat.

She even had my mom fooled.

"I hope she's okay," my mom said. "Do you think she's frightened?"

Sure, I thought. Courtney scared—ha! Maybe in a taller tree, like a giant redwood, she might have been. I looked up and up and up through the tree-tops. The leaves had started to turn fall shades and were tinged light green and gold and orange. Jolly had a colorful feast.

"Don't worry, Courtney, help is on its way!" my mom shouted.

The little crowd with cameras had crept up, and they were all hissing "Shhhh," as if Courtney would fall out of the tree if voices were raised above a whisper.

The trampoline-like net supplied by the fire department was poised in case Courtney tumbled from the tree. I hoped that didn't happen, because she'd give us all heart attacks, but my greatest fear was that Courtney would jump because she'd think that would be fun.

The firefighters had set up a ladder, and one of them was climbing it to fetch Courtney. Again I wondered why no one informed these men that Courtney could have come down the tree any old time she wanted. After all, what goes up must come down.

But I decided there might be a lawsuit if they didn't go up and bring her down. The director could have been sued; Chatham, New Jersey, with its miles of wooded acres and lakes and swamps, could have been sued; Jolly's trainer could have been sued. The firefighter they sent up was cute. I'm sure that fact didn't go unnoticed by my favorite and only second cousin.

As he emerged from the foliage on the treetop, there was supportive applause from the audience.

Courtney was smiling her dazzling all-teeth movie-star grin, so I knew there were more than a few cameras in that small crowd. They had been poised to shoot a giraffe that ran like a gazelle but got a real live stunt and a love story. Girl and giraffe. We all watched as the fire department successfully brought her down to safety. It had been quite a day. COURTNEY'S TALL STORY. That would be the headline if it ever became a headline. Even if one of those amateur photographers sold his photos, I was sure it would never be printed in New York papers—it just wasn't enough of a story. We were safe, or at least, I was safe. Courtney would be disappointed. Maybe Jolly would be, too. I didn't know if he had a publicist or not.

They managed to get Courtney standing on her own two legs like a wobbly colt. The director was falling behind his shooting schedule, and maybe his budget, because after Jolly's trainer calmed Jolly down and revived him with some shrubbery, the director yelled, "Cue Jolly! Quiet on the set! Action! Roll 'em!"

My mom threw a towel around Courtney's shoulders as if she had won a round in a prizefight and made sure she had another egg-salad sandwich.

"Too bad Jolly can't write. Then he would be able to give me his autograph," Courtney said, with a tiny blob of mayo on her chin. But it didn't matter, because even if she'd been through a hailstorm, or had spinach between her teeth, or looked like Rudolph the Red-Nosed Reindeer because of a bad cold, she always looked pretty.

Then Courtney told me about her relationship with giraffes. "I've always admired them from afar," she said dramatically. This was vintage Courtney. I wondered if she planned it or it just came out that way. Courtney then told me in un-Courtney-like fashion, "See, I save everything I can find on giraffes. Back in Beverly Hills I have pins, earrings, a stuffed pillow. But I don't have a real giraffe," she said wistfully.

Well, she did now.

I thought as we climbed in the truck that Courtney had gotten into trouble, big trouble, but it would go unnoticed. I could hold my head high in the halls of I.S. 44. As I smiled at her, I thought of something—Courtney usually got the last laugh. Somehow.

The next morning, as if she knew beforehand, Courtney tiptoed out of our room in her white eyelet nightgown as if it were Christmas morn and opened the door a crack. Then she and Wilheim Von Dog hauled in the Sunday paper, the one that was loaded with pictures.

When I stumbled into the kitchen five minutes later, I could see something had happened by the look on Courtney's face. She was grinning like the Cheshire cat. She had won after all. I admitted defeat.

On the front page of the paper was a picture of her hanging on to Jolly the giraffe's neck. Sure enough the caption read: TALL STORY. My crazy cousin Courtney had done it again! Right about now every single house with kids who attended I.S. 44 who had this particular paper delivered to their door—they all knew.

*"I hear she's her second cousin."*

*"Where's she from? Beverly Hills? Well, they're different out there. The sun does that, and they put something in the pools."*

I was starting to hear voices. My mom made scrambled eggs and bacon, which Howard couldn't finish because he was laughing so hard. They got up his nose, and he was sputtering.

About eleven o'clock, after a call from Joan and then Bernie, the doorbell rang. It was Felicity and Dawn. I opened the door, and they came into the living room, cheering, finishing in splits. We couldn't get Felicity up for a second or two.

"We've got it!" Dawn said, out of breath.

"Yes," Felicity said. "Sue Ellen Fishbein is moving to Florida."

"So?" Courtney and I said together.

"So, there's a spot open on the cheerleading squad, and Courtney's going to be on it! *This* is what her image needs."

They were very careful to add—*not* running up trees chasing after giraffes.

Courtney sat down on the couch, stunned.

"Me, a cheerleader. It's been a lifelong dream," she whispered, as if she were accepting an Oscar. I couldn't tell when she was acting.

"But, Courtney, it will take a lot of hard work," Felicity reminded her.

"Yes."

"We've got to change your image."

"Yes."

"People forget," Dawn said.

"Yes."

I thought Courtney was getting a little carried away; maybe she had a hidden agenda. Maybe she thought she would invite Josh to a game, and while watching her cheer he would fall madly in love with her and stop thinking of her as a slice of pepperoni pizza.

Actually, I never could tell exactly what Courtney was thinking.

# CHAPTER THIRTEEN

The apartment was more like a three-ring circus than ever. Natasha was in the kitchen making a "little something." Courtney was in the living room practicing cheers. In no time at all she had mastered the cartwheel and splits. She was just naturally athletic. I was sure she would make the squad. Plus, she was a movie star. How could they reject her?

Actually I didn't have a chance to have a real heart-to-heart talk with Courtney until that night after Howard and my mom took us to Hung Lo's, their favorite Chinese restaurant. Courtney's autographed picture was taped inside the window right next to other theater, television, and movie stars.

I always ordered the same thing. Moo goo gai pan.

I liked to say it. It was thinly cut strips of chicken that looked like they had been served with vegetables. Courtney was adventurous with food. She would order anything, spicy or nonspicy. She liked it all.

So that night after dinner, we lay on our twin beds, hands on our stomachs—Courtney blowing and popping bubbles—and returned to the subject of the day. Boys.

"Courtney, this is the first time I've had a chance to talk to you," I said. "You're always so busy."

"I'm busy? You're never home. Where do you disappear to?"

We could hear Daisy in the bathroom making chimpanzee noises.

I ignored her question. "About boys?" I began cautiously.

"I kissed him seven times Friday. Sometimes I get so nervous, we have to do it over and over. But I know he likes me. I can sense it."

Well, that was that. I balanced myself on my elbow, the same elbow that kept grazing Wally's elbow, and said as firmly as I could, "Courtney, I want to talk about a boy *I* like." I left out Zach, the boy in the library, because I felt we were just friends and I hadn't seen him all that much. All we talked about were school subjects and biographies.

"That's beautiful," Courtney said, closing her eyes and popping a bright chartreuse bubble.

"What's beautiful?"

89

"You asserted yourself. You got mad at me. You said, and I quote, 'Courtney, I want to talk about a boy *I* like.' You're right, Cath, sometimes I tend to be a tad self-centered. But who wouldn't be with all the attention I get?"

I thought about that. One thing about Courtney, she wasn't overly sentimental.

"Tell me about it," she said. "And we'll figure out a strategy."

Now that made excellent sense to me. I liked plans. I needed everything to be orderly. Becoming Wally's girlfriend could be organized and disciplined so I could see progress every day. Maybe I could chart it with a graph.

"Now, when do you see him?" Courtney asked, rotating some gum from her mouth to the top of her wrist. When she changed flavors this mouth-to-wrist change was almost a certainty. I smelled the essence of Lemon Mist in the air. Courtney had a never-ending supply of gourmet bubble gum just as she pulled her clothes wrinkle-free from her suitcases.

"Only in orchestra, well, in history, too, but he sits behind me so I can't really see him."

"In orchestra where does he sit?"

"We're elbow to elbow."

Courtney mulled that over.

"You could position yourself to bump into him at his locker or try to sit next to him in the cafeteria. You see, Cath, repetition is good, and if he keeps seeing you, he'll notice you. You're so shy he probably doesn't even know your name."

"Of course he knows my name," I said sharply. But Courtney was right. I was a little shy but especially in the Boy Department.

"You know what?" she said. She went through the ritual of changing flavors again, slapping the old one on the top of her wrist and filling the air with the unmistakable scent of Grape-Ade. "I think we should have a boy-girl party if it's okay with your mom and Howard."

"You mean—"

"A boy-girl party," she repeated.

"Is that what you did in Beverly Hills?"

"Oh, no," she said. "I didn't have girlfriends, and most of the boys were already swimming in my pool, so it would have been a waste of potato chips. But here we could do it. Why not? I could invite Josh."

The thought of a party was beginning to excite me. "I could invite Wally." If I could get through the invitation stage, I would be fine. It would be easier to be with him in a group of people.

I rushed to my desk to get a notebook and a pencil.

"I'll have to ask my mom," I said.

"Uh-huh, and I bet she'll say yes."

"I can hand-letter the invitations."

Courtney groaned impatiently. "Cathy, buy them. It's easier and faster. What about music?"

"Well, Wally, this guy I like, has a little band."

"Oh, great, a string quartet."

"No, I think they play dance music," I said.

"Food?"

"Oh, my mom and Howard will take care of that," I said. "Don't worry. It should work out." What could go wrong?

"Yeah, we'll have Josh right here, and I can see if he's interested or not. You'll have Wally here and— his name is really Wally? How could you name a child Wally?" she blurted out.

Suddenly we got the giggles and started rolling around in our twin beds laughing uproariously. I stopped when I saw a crimson robe in the doorway. We both looked up.

"Girls, tomorrow's a school day, and Courtney has to look fresh on the set."

"Mom, can we have a boy-girl party?"

"I don't see why not," she said. "Just as long as Howard and I are here to supervise. We'll talk about it tomorrow. I can make that nice cake from 'Betty's Kitchen.' "

She closed the door, and we put the pillows over our heads to muffle our laughter. We were both remembering when Wilheim Von Dog scampered across the set, and Betty continued to give her cooking lesson.

Courtney sat up and hugged Wilheim Von Dog as she continued to sob with laughter.

"Courtney, are you okay?" I asked through my own tears.

"Couldn't be better," she said, wiping her eyes.

She changed flavors and popped bubbles until I realized all at once that she had fallen asleep with her favorite flavor in her mouth and her dog under an arm.

I stayed awake a little while longer, analyzing the situation. I thought the idea of a party was a good one, especially since it would solve our Josh and Wally problems. We had forgotten to discuss what we would wear. I had my red silk dress. She must really like this guy, Josh, to plan a whole party around him. Courtney was this big movie star, but this was such a normal-type thing to do. Maybe Courtney was changing. But then again Courtney hadn't changed in thirteen years, and one thing was certain, she wasn't normal.

# CHAPTER ═══
## ═══FOURTEEN

I sat in the bleachers in the gym the day Courtney tried out for cheerleading. She was wearing a green sweatshirt and a white pleated skirt, neon green socks, and bright white sneaks. The head cheerleader blew her whistle, and the girls tried out in little groups of three. This was a brilliant scheme, I thought. If she made cheerleading, Courtney would have to stay out of trouble because she wouldn't have time to get into it. As I watched Courtney, I mentally went over our plans for the party. I knew a lot could go wrong. What if Wally decided at the last minute he couldn't come? What if Josh declined the invitation? After all, he was a star. The two guests of honor who wouldn't know they were being

94

honored would be missing. What if there was an early snowstorm and no one could come? Of course, even I didn't think that was a real worry. It wasn't October yet.

"Worry, worry, worry," Courtney had said the night before when we were putting on some clear nail polish. Courtney used to wear shiny pea green, but they stopped making it. "All you do is worry."

She was right. Also, I detested change. I never did anything on impulse. I was brought back to the present by Courtney's awesome one-handed cartwheel. She was great and she really wanted to make the cheerleading squad.

When the coach, the English teacher Ms. Macri, got up to announce who would take Sue Ellen Fishbein's place, Dawn, Felicity, and I hugged one another. Courtney shut her eyes, and I had a vision of her in ten years waiting for her name to be called at the Academy Awards.

"Our new cheerleader is Courtney Green," Ms. Macri announced, and all of us jumped up and down and clapped our hands. I marveled again about how easily everything seemed to come to Courtney except for good grades.

She would be cheering at the next game, which was a week after our party. The big party was this Saturday night. It was all I could think of.

That and Wally. Thank heaven we sent out invitations and I didn't have to ask him. I never would have had the nerve in person.

To say that we invited disaster would be too dramatic, but at the party something happened I never, ever dreamed would happen. Things like that only happened in the movies.

Everything was perfect. The weather report predicted a drizzle, but it never happened. It was a beautiful Indian-summer, early-autumn night. Howard had bought cheese balls, cheddar cheese rolled in walnuts and pecans. Howard still didn't know that much about kids. My mom had baked the cake from "Betty's Kitchen." All the preparations made Wilheim Von Dog overexcited, so we put him in the bedroom with a doggie toy. Courtney made punch—Tropical Fruit Kool-Aid with tiny marshmallows floating in it. We had chips, crackers, pretzels, plenty of ice-cold sodas, and little bowls of M&M's with or without peanuts. I put on a tape of music before Wally arrived, and I was reduced to being a nonfunctioning imbecile. I suddenly hated my crush, but I was stuck with it.

Felicity and Dawn arrived first. Then came Richie, Samantha, and Jennifer. All of the other kids arrived shortly after that. But no Wally. I felt that if someone talked to me, I would scream, I was so nervous. Then the doorbell rang and the doorman announced someone who was coming up. I knew by Courtney's crestfallen face that it wasn't Josh. Come to think of it, Courtney seemed more nervous than I had ever remembered her being. She really liked this guy, but it looked as if she had met her match in him.

Wally and his band, Alphabet Soup, finally showed up and set up in the living room. I was used to seeing Wally play the cello, but now he was playing an electric guitar. He was a musical genius. There was someone playing saxophone and someone with a huge bass and they were all really good. Howard and my mom had pushed the furniture back against the walls so we could dance.

Then I heard uproarious laughter and screaming. Daisy, the chimpanzee, who had taken over the house, had strolled out and wanted to be a part of the party. She grabbed a chunk of chocolate cake and wiped her face with a napkin. I shut my eyes, mortified. She was wearing her pink ruffly dress and had a big pink bow in the tufts of hair on the top of her head. I watched, paralyzed, as my mom rushed in from the kitchen to escort her out of the room. But some of the kids were screaming, "No, let her stay!" and they started to dance with her. Daisy was a good dancer.

When the doorbell rang, I saw Courtney practically jump. I could tell by the ear-to-ear grin on her face that the only person left to arrive was Josh, and that's who it was. I was curious about this Josh who had stolen Courtney's heart and left her a blithering idiot.

When I saw him I couldn't believe it! I opened my mouth, and it wouldn't close. I hadn't invited him. It was Zach from the library. Did I invite Zach? No, of course, I hadn't. I hadn't seen him. Unless Zach had a twin brother named Josh or an identical look-alike.

"Cathy," Courtney said, "I'd like you to meet Josh. He plays opposite me in *Chocolate Ice Cream.* Josh, have a piece of chocolate cake," she cooed.

"Cathy," he said, taking my shoulders and holding me at arm's length. Courtney was talking to Wally, so I guessed it was okay to talk to him. "What are you doing here?"

"I live here," I said. "You said your name was Zach," I said, trying to keep the accusatory tone out of my voice.

"Oh, that," he answered, grinning. Then I noticed he wasn't wearing his wire-rimmed glasses. The ones that slipped down his nose. His eyes were ice blue marbles exactly the way Courtney had described them to me.

"Contact lenses," he said. "Josh Jordan is my stage name. I hate it. I want to be an environmental lawyer. This is my last picture so that I can just be a regular high school student. An ordinary fourteen-year-old. That's why I go to the library to study when I have the time. It's peaceful and quiet. I've been thinking of you."

Well, I didn't want to think about that at all. Courtney liked him. Funny, I didn't think he would be her type. That was what was quirky about crushes.

You never really got to know the person. Zach/Josh was more like me. I liked him, but it was too monumental to comprehend.

I watched Courtney. She was wearing an aqua dress with a scooped neck and a giraffe pin. I, of course, wore my red silk dress for the first time. Wally had set his guitar down to dance with Daisy. Courtney was laughing uproariously. I began to munch on M&M's nervously. I walked away from Zach/Josh because he was Courtney's boyfriend.

Wally's Alphabet Soup band was playing an original song Wally had written called "Veggies." I didn't like it. In fact, I found myself not liking his band. That was strange. Courtney came over. "Super," she said. "Awesome party, Cath."

Courtney walked away and started dancing. She was a fantastic dancer, but then again she did everything brilliantly except her homework.

I was at my own party and didn't know what to do. I couldn't go over and talk to Zach/Josh. Wally was busy with the band. Courtney was dancing with everyone including Daisy. I felt confused.

I only knew my crush on Wally was beginning to evaporate like the scent of Courtney's Lemon Mist gourmet bubble gum. Of course nothing like that would go away in one night, but I realized Zach/Josh was more my type. He was my friend. I liked Courtney's boyfriend. That was the worst thing that ever happened to me, especially since he said he had been thinking of me. Of course, there are all different ways to think of a person or think about a person.

He was standing alone, idly munching on potato chips. I could see why he was alone. The kids knew he was a movie star, and it was too awesome to approach him. Courtney walked up to him, and they started talking.

That was how it should be. Why did I feel like crying? I turned when I heard Courtney's bubbly laugh, which sounded like door chimes. When I turned around, I saw that Zach was gone—probably out the door. I had an urge to run after him, to tell him that it was okay, he would be a normal kid. I looked out the window. That drizzle that was expected had turned into a heavy thunder shower.

Courtney came up to me, her face flushed, out of breath, Kool-Aid stains on her upper lip. "Josh had to leave. What did you think of him?"

"Oh, nice, very nice." Now I was lying. Or was I just leaving out the truth? Something had happened.

"Yeah, nice," she said. "And Wally's very nice."

"I think so," I said crisply. Sometimes I talked that way when I got nervous.

"I expected him to be a little bit of a double dork. But he's a musical genius. Super."

"Super."

Then the party was over. The band was leaving, and my mom and Howard were moving furniture around as Courtney picked the last marshmallow out of the Kool-Aid and Daisy helped herself to the last chunk of cake. I felt somehow that Courtney and I were in trouble again, but I didn't know where it was leading. Our next adventure would make Courtney's romance with Jolly the giraffe look like child's play.

# CHAPTER FIFTEEN

The following week was hectic, and Courtney and I hardly had a chance to talk. I did notice that she was chewing more bubble gum than usual, though never in school, of course. I couldn't put my finger on it, but our relationship seemed strained somehow. Maybe she suspected I had feelings for Josh. Or perhaps it was because the pressure had finally gotten to her. Besides her role in the film and her perfect attendance in school (I was really proud of her for that), she was going to cheer at the Friday night game between our own Green and Whites and the Red and Whites being bused in from Long Island. She had practiced so much I thought she would be too stiff to climb the steps in school.

But Courtney was fine. I wasn't, though, because there was just this tension between us. As soon as the game was over, we would have to have a heart-to-heart.

The gym was filled to capacity that Friday night. Felicity, Dawn, my mom, Howard, and Natasha, and I had first-row seats. The team ran out, and the whole school cheered. Then the cheerleaders ran out and I smiled. Courtney looked smashing. Green and white were her colors, too. Actually, every color was her color. She wore a little green ribbon in her hair.

"Go, Courtney, go!" our little group chanted until we were *shhhh'd* by the row in back of us. I could hear bits of conversation buzzing like flies around my ears.

"She's a movie star," someone said. "Is this a publicity stunt?"

"Must be," another voice said. "How else did she make the squad?"

Now, that made me angry. I turned around and said, "She's my cousin Courtney, and she made the squad because she practiced and deserved to be a cheerleader. I didn't see you at the tryouts."

There was an icy silence.

Finally one of them said, "Well, excuse me."

I began to blush then. I wasn't used to being so firm. Too bad Courtney hadn't heard me. I had asserted myself. I suddenly wondered if Courtney felt awkward going to a normal school. Of course, it *was* New York City and there were plenty of professional kids, but I think most of them went to private schools.

The cheerleaders had picked up their green and white pom-poms and were jumping up and down. The team ran out onto the floor. Our school yelled "Yea!" The kids from Long Island ran out.

I didn't know if I was the first one to see them, but when I did I sensed impending disaster. In the audience were a couple of men with shoulder-supported cameras. They weren't photographing the game, because they had their lenses zeroed in on Courtney.

I looked over at Felicity and Dawn. They had big grins plastered all over their faces. Then I knew what had happened. They had notified the TV stations that Courtney the movie star was Courtney the down-to-earth cheerleader. Courtney was going to get a lot of publicity, and she hadn't generated it. She was drawn to a camera, though, and her smile was dazzling from where I sat.

"Let's see another jump, Courtney!" a cameraman yelled.

"Yeah, smile as you go higher."

I put my face in my hands. This couldn't be happening. I was just so embarrassed. No one could think of anything to say. I could tell that Felicity and Dawn never meant it to become a three-ring circus.

Finally my mom shouted, "Put those cameras down and leave these kids alone."

The basketball teams, green and white and red and white, went into a huddle. Well, it was ruining their game. But the next thing I saw was Courtney running helter-skelter out of the gym and into the hall. Felicity, Dawn, and I rushed out to join her.

"I'm sorry," Felicity said. "We thought it would be good for your image."

Then I saw something that stunned me. I had read somewhere that there were seven wonders of the world. But this was the eighth. My cousin Courtney was crying. A tear was trickling down her cheek.

We all put our arms around her.

"They said I was messing up their game, and they didn't want me on the squad," Courtney said. "This is the first time I've been rejected by a whole group of boys. Boys usually like me." I wondered how much of this had to do with her cool reception by Josh and vowed again to myself never to let her know that I liked him.

Then I saw that all the camera people were coming into the hall searching for Courtney. After all, they had been promised a story. Actress that she was, Courtney flashed a dazzling smile and her tears were gone as quickly as a sudden spring thunderstorm.

We could hear the noise inside the gym. People were cheering, but we didn't know for which team or who was winning.

"That's a great shot," a reporter was saying. "How does it feel to be a normal junior high school student?"

Normal? We could never really make Courtney normal. She was too outrageous. Acceptable, maybe.

"It's awesome," Courtney replied. "Super. I've always wanted to go to school in New York and play, I mean, be a cheerleader."

Someone opened the door and we could hear, "Yea, team!" Courtney looked a little sad then, and I could tell she wanted to be on the floor, but she knew it would ruin the game. So she gave her mini press conference in the hall near a bulletin board that had fall leaves push-pinned on it. "Courtney, how is *Chocolate Ice Cream* going?"

"Oh, ready to melt," she said offhandedly. "We're wrapping it up next week."

For a moment my heart skipped a beat and I felt numb. Why hadn't she said anything? Well, we hadn't had time to talk about much. That meant, though, that Josh would have more free time, and Courtney would fly back to Beverly Hills. And then I hated myself for the emotions I was feeling. Not wanting Courtney to go but wanting Courtney to go because everything was just so mixed up. Basically, I knew Courtney and I had to talk, but I didn't know what to say.

The doors opened and I could hear the cheering more loudly. Our team was winning. Courtney jumped, two legs out, arm in the air, and screamed, "Yea, team!" What happened next was unbelievable. The whole sweaty basketball team came running out and hoisted Courtney on their shoulders and carried her back into the gym.

We ran after them.

"You saved the day, Courtney," one player said.

"Yeah, we could concentrate when you left with your camera crews. So we won. Your leaving made us win." Everyone was chanting.

Courtney was laughing, tossing her coppery curls. I couldn't believe this. My crazy cousin Courtney had done it again.

Wasn't it just possible that they had won the game because they had played well?

My mom and Howard and Felicity and Dawn and Natasha came up to us, and Howard said, "Well, what about a round of ice cream?" Natasha was all in favor of that, and we all trooped out of the gym with Courtney, who had a long trench coat draped over her shoulders like the movie star that she was.

"This is the most fun I've had in a long time," Courtney said. "This and the party."

There must be a catch somewhere, I thought. Fun without getting into trouble? And then I thought about that. Maybe this time a little of me had rubbed off on Courtney. Usually it was the other way around. She was having fun being a normal kid.

Of course she could never have normal tastes in ice cream. Courtney ordered a blueberry crunch, chocolate marshmallow, butter pecan ripple sundae with whipped cream and three cherries. Natasha ordered the same. I stuck to vanilla, and Felicity and Dawn had sorbet.

"I guess you'll be on the news tonight, Courtney," Howard said. Howard was developing crinkly lines around his mouth. I noticed it when he smiled, and he smiled a lot, especially when Courtney was visiting us.

Courtney shrugged. "I have a difficult scene tomorrow. I'll have to go to bed early and miss the news."

We all gaped at her.

"Of course," my mom said. "Courtney works very hard."

I wondered if Courtney was getting sick.

# CHAPTER
## SIXTEEN

*Chocolate Ice Cream* was melting, as Courtney liked to say, and maybe it was my imagination, but Courtney was slightly icy to me. Maybe she suspected that I liked Zach/Josh. Sometimes when I went to the St. Agnes branch of the public library, he appeared. Courtney and I had become overly polite to each other. I watched, silently, as she started packing— not that she had unpacked it all.

I was unprepared for her arrival, and I felt as unprepared for her departure. Everything was changing, and I didn't like change. Daisy the chimp had left with her trainer to appear in her TV sitcom. That would be plenty of bananas for her. My mom was leopard-sitting for a sleek baby leopard that resembled a throw pillow when he curled up on our couch. His name was Irwin. Felicity and Dawn were still hard at work trying to secure major talk shows for Courtney, but it was difficult because Courtney wouldn't be a major motion picture star until the picture came out. Although the publicity was going a long way. Even Natasha had gone on to coach her next assignment. A ten-year-old boy with red hair, freckles, and big blue eyes who specialized in horror flicks.

That left my mom, Howard, and me. I didn't think I could spill my secret. *I like my cousin's boyfriend.*

About two days before Courtney left, my mom asked us to meet her at her office before we went to Hung Lo's for dinner. I couldn't imagine what she wanted. Usually she summoned us because we had gotten into too much trouble.

We went down to her office, which she called Phyllis's New Zoo. It really was new and improved over the first one she had had, Phyllis's Zoo. Lining the walls were glossy photographs of some of her clients: Jolly the giraffe, whom Courtney gazed at fondly; Polly the parrot, who had played in dozens of pirate movies and spoke three languages; dogs that had been used in the Sassy movies; a frightening gorilla who was afraid of his own shadow; and our own Ginger, the pink piglet, and mascot of the office, who slept in her very own wastebasket. Actually she was the fourth Ginger my mom had had. The others had outgrown the wastebasket.

Scottie, my mom's assistant, was typing away on a new computer with a cageful of parakeets chirping above his head.

Courtney let out a low whistle.

"Awesome," she said respectfully and headed straight for Ginger.

"Uh, Courtney, dear," Scottie said. "Watch out, she tends to slither."

"Kootchy, kootchy, koo," Courtney said, tickling Ginger's snout.

I guided Courtney to a chair so she wouldn't be tempted to pick her up.

"Okay, send the girls in," I heard my mom say from her office. Again, I wondered why we were there. "Your mom says you should go in," Scottie said, not looking up from his typing.

What had happened that she couldn't talk to us in the restaurant? I didn't even have a taste for my favorite, moo goo gai pan. In fact, lately I had lost my appetite.

"Now, girls, Howard and I think there's been a gross misunderstanding. I want to have a little discussion with you before dinner."

I didn't know what she meant. Nothing had been gross.

"Courtney will be leaving New York soon, and we want you girls to continue to be the best of friends." She stopped and swiped a Kleenex from a box on her desk. Courtney and I each took one. "You see, you're so like Joan and I were at your age."

Courtney and I sat there, unblinking. What if Courtney knew my secret? What if she found out I had been cheating behind her back in the library with the boy she liked? What if she found out I was pretty sure he liked me, too? How did my mom know all this? She leaned in. On her desk was one earring. The other was on her left ear. I studied her outfit. Navy suit, white blouse, very efficient, very neat.

"Cathy," she said. "Courtney came to me and confessed she likes Wally and he likes her and he's coming to Beverly Hills to visit his uncle during the Christmas vacation."

I was stunned.

"What?" I asked in a semistrangled voice.

"It'll be okay, Cath," Courtney said. "You'll meet plenty of guys when I'm gone."

"But I like Zach/Josh and he likes me. We've been meeting in the library. I didn't know how to tell you."

"What!" Courtney said.

"See I met him in the library, and he had these brown eyes and glasses, and I didn't know he was your boyfriend."

"And Wally called me after the party and asked me out for ice cream."

"I hope you didn't have one of your concoctions."

"No, I had vanilla," she said.

And then we were both giggling and hugging, and my mom was blowing her nose. We could hear Scottie sniffling at the computer.

"You see, girls, when you like boys as friends, it's

112

much better. They're the ones you have things in common with," my mom said.

We nodded happily, both knowing that we'd still have crushes on boys who were wrong for us.

"And boys should never interfere with the special relationship you have with each other."

Well, that was for sure. But they usually did.

Courtney nudged me as we were going out the door. "Cathy, listen, live a little. Forget the moo goo gai pan—try the sweet and sour shrimp."

She had jammed some bubble gum in her mouth. Love that Licorice. She smiled and looked as if she had no teeth.

She was the old Courtney, and I felt pretty terrific myself.

So it was hard to believe the next day, Courtney was leaving and would be home that very day. My emotions were jumbled together, and I felt as if I were eating two opposite-tasting foods like sushi and chocolate-covered frozen yogurt.

Howard, my mom, and I drove Courtney to the airport. Courtney's things had to be shipped. I had bought her a giraffe scarf for a going-away present. Following us was a cab with Felicity and Dawn, both teary-eyed, and Zachary and Wally, who were getting to know each other.

"Do you have enough bubble gum in your carry-on case?" I asked.

"Yep."

"Do you have your ticket?"

"Yep. Cathy, stop taking care of everything. Relax. Enjoy."

I settled back in my seat.

"Do you know where your cello is?"

That did it. We both exploded with laughter. We couldn't stop and we couldn't catch our breath. I would miss these laughing attacks. No one laughed like my cousin Courtney. She laughed with her whole heart and soul. It was contagious.

"Girls," my mom said. "If you don't say goodbye now, you'll have to write a letter."

"Will you write me, Courtney?"

"Sure," she said.

She wouldn't.

Suddenly I sobered up. It was really happening. Courtney was leaving. I touched Courtney's arm as we got out of the car.

"Courtney, it feels like we're sisters."

"Yep," she said.

The cab in back of us had stopped, and out came Felicity and Dawn, still tearful, and Wally and Zachary talking about basketball.

Howard was saying, "Maybe the next time Cathy can visit Courtney in Beverly Hills."

But it was hard to hear him because there was so much commotion inside Newark Airport.

Everyone hugged Courtney goodbye. Wally kissed her on the cheek, and I knew Courtney wouldn't wash her face for a week. Courtney thanked my mom and Howard, and I was proud of her.

Then we stood eye to eye. We were the same height and weight, though of course, she was much prettier.

My mom gave us a shove, and we ended up in each other's arms.

"Courtney, I don't know when I'll see you again. It was so nice sharing a room with you."

"No, it wasn't, Cath. I intruded on your privacy, your cello collected dust, your whole life was a jumble. But we also had fun. We always have fun."

She was right.

"And, Cath, thanks to you, I'm a normal kid movie star."

"You mean?"

"Right. Going to school, the party, the cheerleading. See, I never had a chance to be a really normal kid."

"Does this mean you don't want to be a movie star anymore?" I asked.

She shook her curls fiercely. "Oh, no, no. I love being a movie star. But I had a taste of being a normal kid. I could play a normal kid. And it's thanks to you. You're a normal kid and that's your strength. So don't ever stop, but try the sweet and sour shrimp—just once."

I knew then I was ready to write my biography of my cousin Courtney: MY CRAZY COUSIN COURTNEY GETS CRAZIER. But, I wondered—would anyone believe it?

# About the Author

JUDI MILLER was brought up in Cleveland, Ohio, but lives and writes in New York City. She is the author of *My Crazy Cousin Courtney, My Crazy Cousin Courtney Comes Back,* and *My Crazy Cousin Courtney Returns Again,* all available from Minstrel Books. Judi, who has liked to write since she was nine years old, also writes suspense thrillers for adults.

# SPOOKSVILLE™

- ☐ **#1 The Secret Path** 53725-3/$3.50
- ☐ **#2 The Howling Ghost** 53726-1/$3.50
- ☐ **#3 The Haunted Cave** 53727-X/$3.50
- ☐ **#4 Aliens in the Sky** 53728-8/$3.99
- ☐ **#5 The Cold People** 55064-0/$3.99
- ☐ **#6 The Witch's Revenge** 55065-9/$3.99
- ☐ **#7 The Dark Corner** 55066-7/$3.99
- ☐ **#8 The Little People** 55067-5/$3.99
- ☐ **#9 The Wishing Stone** 55068-3/$3.99
- ☐ **#10 The Wicked Cat** 55069-1/$3.99
- ☐ **#11 The Deadly Past** 55072-1/$3.99
- ☐ **#12 The Hidden Beast** 55073-X/$3.99
- ☐ **#13 The Creature in the Teacher** 00261-9/$3.99
- ☐ **#14 The Evil House** 00262-7$3.99

## BY CHRISTOPHER PIKE

**Available from Minstrel® Books**
**Published by Pocket Books**